HOOK

DEAD TO RIGHTS

MELISSA SNARK

NORDIC
LIGHTS
PRESS

HOOK: DEAD TO RIGHTS

ISBN: 978-1-942193-29-6 (ebook)

ISBN: 978-1-942193-32-6 (paperback)

Cover design by J Caleb Design

Contact Information:

Email: admin@nordiclightspress.com

Nordic Lights Press

PO Box 323

Anacortes, WA 98221

Published in the United States of America.

The author respects trademarks and copyrighted material mentioned in this book by introducing such registered items in italics or with proper capitalization.

This book is a work of fiction. Names, persons, places and incidents are all used fictitiously and are the imagination of the author. Any resemblance to persons, living or dead, events or locales is coincidental and non-intentional, unless otherwise specifically noted.

To my wonderful husband Chris.

ACKNOWLEDGMENTS

I would like to say a huge thank you to Marie Brennan, author of the wonderful A Memoir by Lady Trent series. If not for the feedback and encouragement she offered at FOGcon's writing workshop, it's unlikely I'd have completed *Hook: Dead to Rights*.

This book couldn't have happened without the support (and saintlike patience) of my husband, Chris, and my good friend, Sheryl R. Hayes. They indulged my zany rambling and pirate tangents long after everyone else had fallen asleep.

Thank you to my editors, JD Book Services and Shay VanZwoll of EV Proofreading.

Thank you to Tammy Payne of Book Nook Nuts Proofreading.

"All children, except one, grow up."
~J. M. Barrie, *Peter Pan*

Neverland is a wondrous isle of adventure.

Neverland is a cruel lie.

Children follow Peter Pan believing their dreams will come true—to never grow up.

Surprise, surprise... they never will. The children Peter Pan abducts are murdered or meet a grimmer fate.

I'm the child who escaped Peter's treachery. I've made it my life's calling to rescue the Lost Boys, even those who don't wish to be saved. Now Pan has a schooner he's using to steal even more children. I'm the only one who can stop him.

Call me Hook. I am the master and commander of a pirate ship, and I'll have my revenge on Peter Pan if it's the last thing I do.

CHAPTER 1

Frustration—Reminiscing—Unexpected Surprises

I am ink.

I was dark and messy, and got all over everything I touched, an indelible stain that never came out. Imagine... fingers threaded through wild black hair, a box-braid ponytail weighted with luminous pearl beads, a ruthless smile, and a blue steel hook in lieu of a severed left hand. I loved honey and thunderstorms, lied without compunction, lived without constraints, had a scoundrel's heart and a swashbuckler's flair. As a half-breed—human and mermaid—I belonged neither on land nor beneath the sea, so I carved my place in between. My home was a pirate ship named *Revenge*, her crew was my family, and together we roamed where the wind and waves took us.

My essence was the ink of an unwritten story, longing for the page.

I had a tale to tell, but I didn't know where to begin or how it would end. Of words, I had plenty, all of which sounded eloquent and profound in my head. Once written down, however, they were all wrong. My penmanship was clean and bold and legible, but the words themselves seemed the hackneyed scribblings of a madwoman. Crumpled pages littered the floor; the discarded bodies of repeated failed attempts.

That evening, the delicate strains of William Byrd flowed through the great cabin. The piano—played by Virgil Brown, the ship's minstrel—and our other musical instruments had a dedicated nook alongside the port hull. Mr. Brown would lend a sympathetic ear if I chose to seek his counsel, but I wasn't ready to admit defeat yet. Still I sat there, hunched over the writing table, a prisoner to troubled thoughts.

The empty journal mocked me. I gripped the quill pen like a dagger with thoughts of plunging it into the journal's heart. Oh, it was tempting. I wanted to do so, if only for the satisfaction it would bring. But ruining the book and the pen wouldn't solve my problem. I had a bad habit of destroying that which annoyed me. In fits of anger, I'd sunk ships and maimed or massacred anyone who crossed my path.

An aggravated snarl tore from my throat. I shoved my chair back and rose, thrusting the quill into the canister. Beside it, I found the cup of tea I'd long forgotten. I grasped the china saucer and plucked out the tea ball. The lukewarm beverage hit my empty stomach like a bitter medicinal shot.

With a grimace, I decided I needed something stronger so I ambled over to the bar. The ornate rug depicting the Tuatha Dé Danann absorbed the impact of my steps. The floor covering had been installed at Mr. Brown's request. He claimed it improved the acoustics of the room, though I suspected his primary motive had been to silence a particular creaky plank.

The piano recital suited the serenity of the evening. Through the stern windows, twin scythe moons hung in a sky of few and distant stars. The dark and tranquil ocean absorbed the moonlight.

Virgil painted pictures in sound. With the stroke

of a harp, he could inspire sorrow or reverence. In his hands, a drum became a source of primal dread. I'd never understood how he infused such powerful emotions into song. In comparison, I would always be an amateur. A childhood malady had left me deaf in my right ear, but music was still my passion. I *felt* the rhythm in my bones—it soothed the savage beast that slumbered in my heart. Tonight, however, even Virgil's performance failed to penetrate my malaise.

The music's final notes faded away. A completed song, yet somehow it seemed a commentary on my outburst.

"Do you have something you wish to say, Mr. Brown?"

"I wouldn't wish to seem impertinent, Captain..." Virgil had a tired voice for a tired soul, but spoke without hesitation. He cracked his knuckles, which popped with a loud snap. Mr. Brown wore a raw ruby set in a gold band on his pinky finger, his only accessory. He'd told me once it'd belonged to his father.

I chuckled. "You do not *seem* impertinent. You are."

"Now, Captain Hook, no need to be surly."

"I'm always surly, and you're always so very circumspect with your improper queries into my private matters. I wonder when you'll finally get straight to the point."

"Never, Captain. I am who I am, and I'm too darn old to just up and change that now."

"To listen to you, you've one foot in the grave."

"Well, now. And here I thought I had both feet firmly planted there," he said with a wry chuckle.

At the bar, I filled two tumblers with brandy. I raised one, shut my eyes, and inhaled. Good brandy must be savored before it's tasted. This was smooth and mild, a complex scent slowly unfurling. I raised a tumbler toward Virgil in a wordless offer, but he shook his head.

"Please pass me my medicine, Captain." Mr. Brown indicated a vial of salve on the bar with a trembling hand. He always shook except when he played, and then magic happened. The moment he caressed ivory keys or stroked vibrating strings, he was strong and steady. His competence extended beyond stringed instruments to wind. Those old lips breathed life into flutes and trombones.

I fetched the vial and removed the stopper since he always struggled with fine tasks. I nested the vial safely in his gnarled fingers. Afterward, I eased away to give the man his space. Despite his frailties—

because of them—he took pride in his self-sufficiency.

"Do your hands hurt?"

"My hands always hurt."

Ask a stupid question... I sipped the brandy. It slid down my throat, smooth liquid flame with an underlying note of blackberry.

He poured infused oil into his palm and rubbed his hands together. A sweet, woody aroma laden with notes of pine and lemon infused the air. *Frankincense.* I couldn't smell it without thinking of Virgil. He personified a weary traveler, brimming with cynicism and wonder. Bright eyes and a scalp as smooth as a tumbled stone. A gentle soul, rarefied tastes, more than a little holy.

Virgil corked the vial and set it atop the piano. "I'll take that brandy now, if the offer's still open."

"Of course." I brought the second tumbler to him and settled on the bench beside him. In companionable silence, we indulged together.

Eventually, he cleared his throat. "So, knowing I'll take your secrets into the great beyond when I go, tell me your troubles."

"There'll be no great beyond for you, Virgil. You'll transform into music when you pass." I spoke without thinking and endured immediate regret.

The crew would, no doubt, interpret such insipid nonsense as a sign of softness. I guarded constantly against showing even a hint of weakness. For both pirates and sharks, the scent of blood led straight to a feeding frenzy.

Virgil's jaw dropped. A profound and uncomfortable silence settled. To break it, I lurched off the bench and strode to the bar to pour another shot. Amber liquor sloshed into the tumbler, poetic and beautiful in its motion.

"Why thank you, Captain Hook, I'm flattered. I rather like the idea of being immortalized in my music."

"Don't go around telling others I said that."

"Of course not, I promise." He raised a hand in pledge.

I believed him, but not from blind faith in his integrity. In large part, the old man's prosperity depended on my patronage. On a pirate vessel, a musician constituted an unnecessary extravagance. Other captains had mistresses—I had a minstrel, and I kept him well.

Brandy and confidences flowed, and Virgil regaled me with a story about storytelling. Then an urgent rap sounded on the cabin door. A flush of annoyance warmed my skin. I glanced at Virgil, who gave an exaggerated shrug. Before I called out, the entrance flew on its hinges and smashed into the bulkhead.

First Mate David Starkey burst through the entrance. Breathing heavily, he bent forward so his long tiger-striped hair hung in his face. He had a predator's unwavering regard: gleaming green eyes with vertical-slit pupils. Orange and black stripes ran through his tousled hair, and continued along triangular sideburns to his jawline. In addition to cat's eyes, he had high, pointed ears, and the contours of his lower face suggested a muzzle. The animal traits were souvenirs from his years as a Lost Boy. Every child who had kept company with Pan eventually acquired the characteristics of a beast. Rumor held many of the wild creatures that dwelled in the Neverland Woods had once been children.

"Captain, I've sighted a ship!"

CHAPTER 2

Dangerous Obsessions—Unfortunate Tykes

In a smooth motion, I rose from my chair. Mr. Brown remained seated, as well he should. Aside from a pirate ship being his place of residence, matters of piracy were not his concern. Point in fact—I disliked subjecting an artist of his accomplishment to the cold brutality of the trade.

"Is it a mercantile vessel?" I asked Starkey. Naturally, I assumed he'd breached protocol for good reasons—a ripe prize, for instance.

Revenge earned a living preying on the vessels that strayed into the Neverland Sea. They hailed from around the world, representing a dizzying range of people and cultures. Perhaps the Devil's triangle pulled them through, or their course crossed dead waters. I'd studied it for years, but there was no discernable pattern, and thus no way to predict when or where one would appear. Such ships could vanish in a matter of seconds, so initiative became imperative. We maintained a constant state of readiness because minutes might make all the difference between loss and victory. If luck sided with us, this would be an East India Company fleet carrying tea or silk, both of which could be sold to the faerie folk for a good profit.

Starkey gathered himself, and instinctively I tensed. He thrust out his chest, and said the words for which I long and dread to hear. "No, Captain. It's Peter Pan."

Peter Pan.

I inhaled sharply. The mere mention of Pan's name breathed fervor into my obsession. A fire lit within me. Its flames seared away my thin veneer of humanity, exposing the savagery lurking in the depths. Starkey met my gaze, his tiger eyes aglow with ferocity. He had seen me at my best and my worst. We're kindred souls, he and I.

Mr. Brown, however, had a sensitive soul in need

of nurturing and protection, especially from the likes of me. Reflexively, I glanced at the musician.

He tipped his chin and smiled. "I believe it's time I retire, Captain. My old bones are tired."

"Good evening, Mr. Brown." I offered a curt nod.

"A good evening to you and Mr. Starkey, too.'

"Good night, Mr. Brown," Starkey returned with a lift of his whiskers. He gave the distinct impression of laughter, even though his tenor remained perfectly civil. He *always* appeared smug enough to beg smacking.

T'was part of his charm.

Pleasantries completed, I strode toward the entrance. Starkey had already wheeled. I followed on his heels and hurried to catch up. Annoyance edged my mood, because I sensed Starkey was withholding something important from me.

When we drew even in the passageway, I sidestepped, ramming my shoulder and elbow into his side. Starkey grunted and pushed back. The contest turned into a brief wrestling match. He and I stood about the same height; which was to say, I was taller than most men. Starkey had dense muscles and a full build, where I was long and lean. Neither of us were fully human, however, so our superior strength was an even match.

"What makes you think Pan is aboard this ship you've sighted?"

He chuckled. "You'll see."

"Maybe I don't want to see. Tell me." I shoved him against the bulkhead and pressed the smooth curve of my hook against his throat. A dense, dark, fragrant aroma surrounded him, and I could have identified him in total darkness by scent alone.

His hot breath huffed across the bare skin of my throat and his claws scraped across my forearms without breaking the skin. Such aggression from anyone else would've triggered my worst impulses, resulting in a bloody mess on the deck. But such was our trust.

We've been together *that* long.

"Telling you will do no good. You're too much of a cynic. You won't *believe* until you verify the truth with your own eyes." Starkey shook with the force of his silent snickering.

Blast it. He was right. He knew me *that* well.

I released and pushed him ahead. "Show me, then."

"Aye, Captain," he said, still laughing. He never stopped, not really.

Together, we ascended through the companionway to the poop deck, located behind the mizzenmast. The moment I set foot on deck, I pivoted, assessing the ship's status and conditions. Over time, the performance of such evaluations became ingrained in the psyche of a successful naval commander. The final hour of the First Watch found the night clear and dark, the seas silky smooth, and a steady tailwind blowing at about fifteen knots.

Revenge was a warship designed for stealth and combat. Five hundred tons of grace and power, a hundred sixty feet long from bow to stern, thirty-two at her beam. Four masts supported six black sails. Her hull was constructed from ebonized oak and her decks were prized teakwood. On moonless nights, she vanished from view—shadows layered over shadows.

She had fangs and claws, this lovely vessel of mine: twenty-eight cannons, sufficient firepower to blast the gates of Hades off their hinges, and a crew of seventy bloodthirsty buccaneers. We were a veteran warship. The gun crew had affection and admiration for our artillery. Each cannon had a name engraved on its trail and the crew spoke as though the guns were people. "Oh, Jumping Jack has a real kick today," they'd say. Or, "Talia, she's my favorite gal, always fires straight and true, she does."

We sailed northeast toward Neverland. Mr.

Smee, the Irish bo'sun, manned the helm, gripping the wheel in his chubby fingers. From the highest point in the rigging to the lowest depth in the hold, the mood of the ship churned with restlessness. The many eyes and ears of the crew sensed something amiss.

"Evening, Captain," Mr. Smee called out in a voice quivering with anxiety, presumably over my appearance on deck at such an odd hour. Admittedly, I seldom broke from my routine, but it took little for the man to work himself into a tizzy. A spot of bother reduced him to jitters.

"As you were, Mr. Smee," I responded.

"Aye, Captain," Mr. Smee said, heaving a loud sigh.

Starkey snickered and pitched his voice for my ears alone. "How that man ever became a pirate is beyond me."

"You know how," I snapped, flushed with irritation. Of course I agreed, but wouldn't say so aloud, not where I might be overheard.

Mr. Smee lacked the mental toughness and the physical robustness necessary for the buccaneer career, and I would have long ago insisted he retired... if circumstances had differed. As things stood, however, the Irish bo'sun was a valuable member of the crew. I needed Mr. Smee's expertise, not only with the care of lines and rigging, but in the stewardship of children who invariably adored him. So he stayed, secure in his post.

Starkey stalked across the deck toward the starboard. Without pause, he swarmed up the ratlines into the rigging. He navigated the canopy in lithe leaps and bounds, always fearless, cat-confident in his dexterity. I seized a rope and ascended the shroud, though with far less grace and speed.

The first mate arrived at the mizzenmast first. He clung to it, the claws of his four paws sunk deep in the wood. Starkey wore a loose-fitting linen shirt and breeches without boots. His tail lashed behind him, a whip without a crack. The short, thick fur that covered his body stood on end and his muscles bunched when he gathered his strength. He sprang, kicking off backward, and soared.

The leap launched him in a high arc through the span between the sails. Mid-flight, he performed a one-eighty turn. He caught the main mast with all fours, gouging a spray of splinters with his claws. He exemplified poetry in motion.

"Show off," I muttered and grinned. I freed a line and swung over to the main mast, and then climbed to join him in the crow's nest. Perhaps I arrived slower, but I got there eventually and in one piece.

When I swung my leg over the rim of the basket, a sharp snap came from the floor. I glanced down and discovered the end of a broken ruler protruding from beneath my boot. Scattered charts and navigational aids littered the platform, including a compass and a sandglass. I nudged the clutter aside to avoid causing further damage. Chaos was intrinsic to David's nature—the same way he adored napping and boxes.

Starkey preferred a nocturnal schedule—he took First Watch and Middle Watch (back to back), and held his vigil in the rigging. He sketched star charts at night, oceanscapes by daylight, and always kept the nub of a pencil tucked in his pocket. On a braided hemp cord, he wore a gold brooch: a pair of scrolled lilies framing an oval tiger's eye. The pendant sat at the base of his throat; its gold and brown hues blended into his plush fur.

"Show me this ship," I said, facing out into the velvet night. That evening, the stars were few and far away, little more than faint orange flickers in the sky. Many bright and wandering moons lurked hidden behind the veil.

Starkey raised his arm and pointed. "There, Captain. Off the starboard bow."

"I see it."

On a dark sea, the lights of a vessel shone like a beacon. Indeed, it would have been impossible to miss. That ship of fools had a dozen lanterns or more lit up despite this being one of the murkiest nights of the month.

As if scary things didn't lurk in the dark.

"We're too far out to be certain, but based on her profile, she's small and swift. We'll have to sneak up on her," I said.

Starkey flashed feline fangs, aglow with the excitement of the hunt. "I've ordered all unnecessary lighting doused and the rest dimmed. It'll lessen the chance we'll be spotted."

"Good work," I said and signed simultaneously.

Until then, our conversation had involved a combination of speech and British Sign Language, which I'd known since childhood. I'd met Starkey shortly after Peter Pan brought me to Neverland, and David and I had forged an immediate bond. I'd taught him to sign, and later, reading and writing. He'd trained me in hand-to-hand combat, tracking, and trap building. We'd made a deadly team right from the start. Stealth and unspoken communication had given us a definitive advantage in the island's competitive—and often lethal—games. Years later, the entire crew of *Revenge* understood and utilized sign language on a regular basis. Among pirates, hearing impairment was a common condition resulting from the deafening explosions of cannon fire. Of course, the crew always plugged their ears with wax, but damage to the delicate inner ear was cumulative and inevitable.

The other ship was too far away to discern any clear details, so I dug out my brass spyglass, designed for one-handed use. It had been a gift from a former lover, and counted among my most valued possessions. Through its lens, I appraised our quarry across the nautical miles separating the two vessels.

My initial assessment proved accurate. The sleek schooner was fifty-three-feet long, ten at her beam. Sharp lines built for speed and three tall-sparred masts, rather than the two common to a vessel of her class. She would be swift, but have small cargo holds. Assuming her crew to be minimally competent, I estimated the vessel capable of achieving a staggering top speed of eighteen knots. In comparison, *Revenge* averaged seven to eight knots; a maximum of ten, but only when conditions were optimal.

Starkey lingered at my side. He always

understood and respected my need for silence, a quality I valued in a companion. Like me, David appeared to be in his mid-twenties and had for decades. In our youths, Starkey and I had both been touched and transformed by faerie magic—though in different ways—into something other than fully human. We'd grown up, but we hadn't grown old. In the very beginning, it hadn't been apparent, but as the years wore on, and those around us grew grayer and frailer, the truth became undeniable. It'd become yet another tie binding us together, however, we stayed together through choice. Starkey had followed me throughout our tumultuous youth and the ensuing years, though I never fully understood why. His loyalty didn't come easy or without question. He challenged me at every turn, but he'd proved true when it counted.

I tucked the scope into the pouch on my belt, and slid a sidelong glance toward the first mate. "That ship is too far out to make out any of her crew, even through the spyglass."

A question begged the asking: what had led Starkey to conclude Peter Pan was aboard the schooner? Put bluntly, what use would the flying boy have for a ship? The immediate and obvious answer left me feeling ill. Vessels were used to transport cargo and people. Pan had no use for freight, but he often ferried abducted children from the Otherworld to Neverland.

"That's so." Starkey caught my gaze and grinned, flashing gleaming sharp incisors. His boldness confirmed my suspicions. He wanted me to make inquiries, but he knew I wouldn't until I'd exhausted every avenue to attaining the solution on my own.

The minutes ticked past while I considered. At last, I asked, "Was the splash impressive?"

"The splash?" Starkey parroted, but disappointment crossed his face. An *ah-ha* blaze of inspiration rushed through me.

"When Pan's ship fell out of the sky. Was the splash impressive?"

Starkey's ears drooped, giving him away. Poor fellow, his poker face was nonexistent. He sighed and swung his hand. "The wave was tremendous. How did you know?"

I allowed myself a small smile. It'd proven to be an evening filled with delightful surprises. Maybe, just maybe, the fickle tides of fate had finally turned in my favor. "Intuition, David. It's why I'm captain, and you're first mate."

David snorted, and I chuckled.

"Where Peter goes, Tinker Bell follows, leaving a

shimmering trail of pixie dust. That vessel is overly bright, even for having every lantern on board lit. It's sitting dead in the water, sails flaccid. There's only one possible reason for Pan to be stranded on a flightless vessel."

"What's that, Captain?" David asked, breathless with awe.

"Unhappy children, Mr. Starkey. Unhappy children."

CHAPTER 3

We Are Pirates

"All hands on deck!" The midnight call spread through the ship in hisses and whispers. Pirates rolled from their bunks and swarmed onto the deck. In accordance with the tenets of stealth, lighting was kept to a bare minimum. We gathered, furtive figures, thieves in the night.

Although neither Starkey nor I had announced the reason for the meeting, somehow the crew knew anyway. A spark of gossip lit a wildfire that burned through *Revenge*—across the decks, upward into the rigging, and downward through the hold, penetrating every nook and cranny.

"We're hunting Peter Pan," the crew hissed. "The captain has the scent. Blood in the water. *Blood in the water*. We're heading into battle."

The fo'c'sle—located at the front of the ship, behind the bowsprit—provided the dais from which I reigned. I stood against the railing, the foremast behind me, and surveyed the crew gathered down on the main deck. Starkey flanked me to the left, mirroring my stance. The first mate had the reflexes down, and certainly the experience to stand the title of master and commander of his own vessel. He only lacked confidence... or perhaps it was motivation. Time would tell whether his ambition proved equal to his innate talent.

Restlessness marked *Revenge's* mood. Starkey and I weren't the only ones on board that nurtured a long-drawn grudge against Pan: several members of the company were former Lost Boys. The men and women had the mood of an unruly mob. They produced quite the brouhaha—dissension and shoving—anger roiling on the verge of boiling over. Make no mistake, however, this crew might appear boisterous and undisciplined, but they were also veteran sailors and soldiers. *Revenge's* crew had the hearts and souls of lions: the fiercest and most ferocious buccaneers in Neverland.

Under my stern regard, their agitation was doused. A hush crashed over their number with the unexpectedness of a white squall. Despite the quiet, I stayed my tongue until the pin-ping silence blanketed the ship. The crew held their bated breath as one united body.

"As many of you already suspect, I believe Peter Pan is aboard the brightly glowing schooner on the horizon," I said. "Mr. Starkey observed its precipitous descent from the clouds approximately a half hour ago. There is one reason and one alone for Pan to have commandeered a ship: he's using it to ferry abducted children from the Otherworld to Neverland."

An uneasy murmur rife with speculation murmur swept through the crew. I paused while it ran its course. From their expressions, many wanted to make inquiries, but of course, it was Mr. Smee who possessed the temerity.

"Your pardon, Captain Hook!" Smee thrust his hand skyward as though he was a school-age lad. Contrary to the core, Mr. Smee carried a bullseye lantern, the lens turned toward him. Of all the crew, he alone stood in a pool of light. Naturally, he didn't wait for permission to proceed. "But why do you suppose the schooner fell?" he asked. "From the clouds, you say?"

At my side, Starkey shifted. We traded a glance, he and I, and arrived at an unspoken agreement that he should take the helm. Coming from him, the tale we were about to tell had a better chance of being accepted without question. Put bluntly, Starkey was the infinitely superior fast-talker.

Starkey is tigerwood: exotic, beautiful, and strong. If *Revenge* were a tree, he dwelled in the heartwood. Where the crew feared me, they shared a rapport with David. He was well liked—one might even say beloved—and respected. If any officer could ever replace me as captain, it would be him.

Starkey drawled, "Everyone already knows this so I shouldn't have to say it, but Beaver's got a memory like a sieve—"

"Hey! Not my fault I caught a cannon ball in the head!" Beaver protested and the crew rained down catcalls and coarse chuckles. Now, Beaver happened to be one of those former Lost Boys I mentioned. As a child, he'd made an unfortunate choice in his animal-hide costume; he had the buckteeth and flat tail to prove it.

"Is so your fault! I warned you to duck!" Cairstine

Wright, my chief engineer, slapped Beaver on the back, sending him stumbling, and the others cackled like jackals.

Starkey joined them, cultivating their camaraderie in a way I could never match, only envy. Quicksilver, his demeanor grew stern. His intent tiger-stare intimidated them into silence again.

He continued, "For that ship to fly, it'd require two things: pixie dust and happy children. The schooner has the glow of pixie dust, which has led the captain and I to conclude that unhappy children are the reason she can't fly."

"This is terrible! Why are those children unhappy?" Smee wore a terrible frown at the very thought of those poor, unfortunate souls. The bo'sun waved his chubby arm so the folds of flab jiggled.

Irritation prickled my skin. It probably never crossed Smee's mind to be grateful for our good fortune. For us pirates—and would-be saviors of the Lost Boys—this supposed ship of sorrows provided a golden opportunity to snatch those children from Peter's clutches. I parted my lips to issue a reprimand, but Starkey caught my elbow. He squeezed ever so gently. The subtle intrusion brought me to my senses.

"Illness, no doubt," I grated from between clenched teeth.

Smee rounded his expression—eyes and mouth. "Illness?" he parroted. "What sort of illness?"

Ah, but am I a wretch? I derived no small pleasure from Smee's distress. If anything, his agitation inspired a certain sadistic satisfaction. "Quite possibly a plague or a pox. It seems unlikely one sick child would be enough to bring down the entire ship."

"A pox!" Mr. Smee paled. Fright crossed his face, but not a hint of doubt. He accepted the explanation without question.

The beauty of our contrived cover story resided in its plausibility. It may very well have been the truth. The fact was, Starkey and I had no way of knowing one way or the other. What mattered, though, was convincing Mr. Smee—and the rest of the crew—that we believed wholeheartedly that the schooner was a plague ship.

Tension coiled tightly. The crew hardly said anything but the muffled din bore an ominous tone. Their movements were executed with a certain stiff rigidity. There were few things pirates feared. A virulent sickness, capable of infecting an entire crew who lived and worked in close quarters, however, could provoke dread in even the most hardened seaman.

My hook settled over the round top of the railing. I leaned out to address the company. "In the past, we've pursued Peter Pan at great peril to life and limb. It should come as no surprise to you that I intend to board that ship and rescue those children regardless of the risks. Dr. Chopp..."

"Here, Captain!" Beverly Chopp called out from the quarter deck. The ship's surgeon was a forbidding, steel-haired German woman built like a cannon barrel. When aroused, the force of her temper had an artillery blazing blast. She owned a daunting array of instruments: tools for piercing and puncturing, honed blades, and hefty saws... The mounted collection took up the entire bulkhead of the ship's sickbay.

"The ship's infirmary is too small and centralized," I said. "You'll need to prepare an emergency triage center. We'll set up the secondary infirmary in an isolated section of the cargo hold."

"I shall oversee it." Dr. Chopp dropped her chin.

"The sick youngsters will be brought directly to you and kept under strict quarantine to minimize the chance of the illness spreading," I said to the doctor. "To contain the sickness, we'll have to establish and maintain strict isolation. No one will be allowed to enter or leave the infirmary until I rescind the quarantine."

"Very good," she said. "I'll need assistants to act as caretakers."

"We'll find volunteers." I scanned the grim figures of my crew. Their stances were stiff and straight—corpses in the coffin. They were scared. *Good.* We wanted—needed—them to be wary. It'd keep them alert and obedient, less likely to slack off or challenge an order.

Starkey stepped neatly into the opening in the conversation. "This is a deadly, dangerous undertaking involving a virulent, highly communicable disease. The captain and I have discussed this at length."

My brow rose. We'd done no such thing. The first mate had gone completely off script with his current grandstanding. I hoped he knew what he was doing. I trusted Starkey enough to stand back and let him run with it.

"Therefore, this mission is voluntary," Starkey continued. "Anyone who wishes no part in it may leave. We'll prepare the dinghy with enough food and water to last for a week. From our present position, Vega's Cay is a two-day voyage. Rackham's

Cay is three. The captain and I both pledge on our honor there'll be no retribution taken."

The ensuing silence was startlingly loud. Shadows cloaked the crew, who remained as still as the wooden backdrops used in theater houses. Silhouettes: shapes without substance. Any buccaneer that refused to participate in a raid on an unarmed vessel or abandoned a ship that wasn't sinking wasn't worth his salt. His or her reputation would be ruined—forever branded craven. No captain would take on a coward or a quitter. Even without being able to see their faces, I knew my people well enough to gauge their reactions. They were thoroughly insulted—and shocked.

I was shocked. How dare the first mate bandy about my word, making promises I'd never agreed to uphold? A low hiss forced its way through my clenched teeth. "Starkey..."

He pivoted on his rear paw to face me. Our gazes locked. Starkey and I had been together so long we shared an exceptional rapport. He often knew—or accurately assumed—what I was thinking. I only wished his motivations were half as discernable. His gaze sparkled with mirth and curiosity. That consideration turned into a duel of wills—and a wordless exchange.

What are you up to, David?

He smirked and shrugged. *Wait and see.*

I glared. *I'll skin you alive and use your hide for a rug.*

His grin widened. *I know what I'm doing. Trust me.*

Did I? Trust him with my reputation? Now there was a real clincher. I put that very question to myself, and the debate lasted longer than expected. Not less than a heartbeat, but no more than two. *Of course I did.* And even if his gambit should fail and the entire crew deserted, I'd honor any promises Starkey made on my behalf.

A captain's word is her bond.

Despite this decision, my disposition was far from sanguine. Starkey had deliberately put me in a compromising position and forced my hand. The resulting flare of foul temper required an outlet. When I twisted away from my first mate, my regard fell upon the hapless Smee.

My roar would've done a dragon proud. "Mr. Smee!"

With a startled wail, Smee threw up his hands and staggered. The lantern crashed to the main deck, landed on its side, and rolled. The rotating beam of light cut through the darkness, glancing eerily over people and objects.

A snarl of irritation wedged in my throat. So help me, if Smee set fire to my ship, all bets were off. I'd strap him to an anchor and send him straight to Davy Jones's locker.

Smee windmilled his arms and tipped over. One of his fellows propped up his shoulders and saved him from the fall. Another sailor recovered the lamp and thrust it into the bo'sun's grip.

Smee clutched the lantern to his chest and straightened his crooked spectacles. He quaked and his voice quavered. "Yes, Captain?"

"Shall I reserve a seat on the dinghy for you?"

The bo'sun drew a sharp breath. As expected, he took immediate offense to the suggestion. Now, Mr. Smee and I disliked each other wholeheartedly. Likewise, no love was lost between the first mate and the bo'sun. Owning that, I would add this: Mr. Smee would *never* place his own well-being ahead of a child's. To suggest otherwise construed a grievous insult.

Smee swelled like a pufferfish. "Captain Hook, I'd like to be the first to volunteer to assist Dr. Chopp in the infirmary. In fact, I insist!"

"Well then, if you insist." I gave a modest tilt of

my head to convey surprise, but Starkey overplayed his role. He twitched his ears and lashed his tail, whacking my back in the process. It took an act of self-discipline on my part not to take a swing at him.

"I do insist!" Smee pulled himself up to his full, though trifling height. He garnered cheers and props from the crew who rallied about him.

Right then and there, inspired by the Irishman's courage, three others volunteered to work in the infirmary. More importantly, no one else spoke of leaving. Not a single word. The thing had become *an impossibility*—deliberated on and rejected by the crew. If there had been a holdout, I suspect they'd have found themselves tossed unceremoniously overboard by their mates.

I leaned out over the railing and shouted orders, "Get to it, then! Speak to Dr. Chopp for your assignments. There's much to be done and no time to waste. If anyone assigned to the infirmary should set foot on deck, I'll have you shot and hung! Mr. Mullins, I want you manning the helm. Everyone else, report to your posts! We're sailing in pursuit of that schooner!"

The assembly broke up. Some scurried like mice, others proceeded at a more measured pace, but all obeyed. *Revenge* bustled with activity.

"That worked brilliantly. Exactly as we planned," Starkey said in a voice pitched for me alone.

"Not exactly. *You* went off script."

Starkey flattened his ears. "Not on purpose.... We knew boarding a potential plague ship wasn't going to go over well with the crew. It occurred to me no one would consider desertion or mutiny if we could swing Smee's support."

"It was a smart move," I conceded, though grudgingly. "You're lucky it didn't backfire. Next time warn me in advance."

"I would've, but the thought just popped into my head so I decided to roll with it..." Starkey appraised my scowl and chuckled. "I promise, I'll warn you next time."

"I believe you mean that," I said with a snort. The same as I trusted he would immediately forget his promise the next time a brilliant scheme crossed his path.

"The crew is united and Mr. Smee is out of the way," Starkey pointed out with a proud, conspiratorial gleam. No amount of lecturing on my part would've dampened his cheerfulness.

"True." Mr. Smee could be a caviling carper when events transpired with which he did not agree. If I'd attempted to send Smee to the infirmary, it'd have aroused his suspicions. This way, he'd not only gone willingly, he'd done so at his insistence. Now, Starkey and I were free to do what had to be done. After pondering, I added, "Have six armed sentries stationed outside the infirmary. If anyone asks, say they're there to protect the infirmary... and enforce the quarantine."

"Standard precautions?"

"Yes. When the time comes to board that schooner, make sure every last member of the crew has their ears plugged with wax, especially the boarding party."

"Aye, Captain." Starkey jerked his chin. As a boy and a man, he had experienced the compelling enchantment of Pan's voice many times. He understood how Peter mesmerized and mystified. Earplugs would protect the crew's hearing from more than cannon fire; it'd also shield them from Pan's hypnosis.

"You understand what's expected. That's all."

Starkey performed a quarter turn, but hesitated. "Shall I have Gun Captain Turnkey report to you for instructions?"

"No. We don't want to draw unnecessary attention. Pass the word along quietly. Turnkey is to have the ship's cannons prepped and on standby.

Now cease your infernal lollygagging and get to work!"

"Aye!" Laughing, Starkey took himself off.

Bristling with anticipation, I made my way aft and ascended to the poop deck, or alternatively, the observation deck. It was the aftermost and the highest level of the ship and formed the roof over the navigation room.

From there, my voice rang out across the ship. "Run up the Black!"

With great enthusiasm, the crew took up the order and repeated it as a chorus, "Run up the Black!"

The flag had a white skull and crossbones on a black field. As common practice, pirate vessels intent on attack flew the Black, also known colloquially as the Jolly Roger. The banner inspired universal fear and respect, but it also held an implicit promise: surrender, and your lives will be spared. As a breed, pirates craved profit, and the best take came with the least effort. Murdering merchants served no useful purpose. If anything, it was rather like killing the goose that laid those golden eggs.

The Black was hoisted high and the crew cheered.

The hunt had commenced.

CHAPTER 4

"Full of vexation come I, with complaint."
~Shakespeare, *A Midsummer Night's Dream.*

Through the course of the night, *Revenge* pursued our quarry. The trim schooner demonstrated such odd, inexplicable behavior. For a time she stayed her course, skimming the crested waves. Her square rig of crisp white sails billowed in the stiff wind. She gathered speed, increased her lead. Then, inexplicably, she tacked her sails and dumped her momentum. The gap narrowed. Three times we'd almost come within boarding range, but then she'd caught the wind again and dashed away. The erratic flip-flops complicated and dragged out the hunt.

The schooner mocked and taunted us—and our vexation mounted until *Revenge* roiled with the pent-up frustration of her captain and crew. The ship was a volcano of molten tension on the verge of eruption. They smelled blood and thirsted for a taste. For my part, the marrow in my bones ached. The quest to destroy Pan had informed my decisions for decades. My soul would never know peace until he was no more.

All night, I had maintained a constant vigil on the poop deck, observing the schooner through my spyglass. The crew came and went in shifts, but there I remained. Because I *knew*, due to conviction born of paranoia and prior experience, the moment I stepped off the deck, Peter Pan would escape. Given the many prior occasions when the eternal boy had slipped through my fingers, I refused to risk it. Not while the opportunity to finally bring our long feud to an end was within my grasp.

Dawn threatened—a faint halo on the horizon. Foreboding crushed my chest. Daylight would expose our presence and pursuit to the schooner. The anticipation and dread at the revelation ate at me. I fretted over the schooner escaping, and I second-guessed my conviction that Peter Pan was aboard her.

The current changed, and Eurus—the east wind—exhaled hard and blustery. I tugged down the brim of my cavalier hat, turned up the collar of my jacket, and tucked my chin to my chest against the nippy bite.

"Mr. Mullins," I called down to the helmsman, "alter our course three points forward of the starboard beam."

"Aye, Captain." Charles Mullins turned the ship to her new heading. The second mate was a staid and steadfast man who was obsessed with details and order. He had a dark rosacea rash on his brow, nose, and cheeks. His ears were crooked, the left higher than the right. Paradoxically, he walked with a limp due to his right leg was shorter than its mate. The crew called him, affectionately, Charlie Cattywampus, because every pirate must have a colorful moniker...

Except those who don't.

Truly, Mullins lacked the imagination, daring, and panache necessary to become a pirate. I had brought him on board despite this because he was a skillful navigator and an impeccable bookkeeper. As a rule, Starkey slacked off on his recordkeeping, and on those rare occasions when he could be bothered to maintain something other than a star chart, his handwriting was near illegible. Mr. Mullins performed the first mate's duties and his own—maintaining the essential logs—willingly, without complaint, and so his post on *Revenge* was secure.

"Starkey," I began, canting to address him only to discover he was no longer where I'd thought. *Confounded cat...* I bit off a curse and expelled a thin sigh.

Through the long hours, Starkey had kept me company... at intervals. Sometimes he stood on deck at my side; often he hung in the shroud, close enough for us to converse. But then, without a word or warning, he wandered off, vanishing without a trace. Ten or twenty minutes, or perhaps an hour later, he reappeared, acting as though he'd never left.

A large blur caught the corner of my eye and I came close to ghosting out of my skin. Starkey dropped out of the rigging. He landed on all fours with a solid thump. I dropped the spyglass and my cutlass cleared its scabbard before I checked myself.

Starkey picked up the scope and offered it,

exuding an air of innocence that I didn't buy for a second. "I believe you dropped this, Captain."

I sheathed the cutlass and snatched the spyglass from him. Lucky for him, a thorough examination revealed no damage to the instrument. To double check the internals, I aimed the long glass at the horizon and gazed through it.

Right then, the schooner banked into a tight turn to the starboard side, looping around in a yet another random maneuver—one of many—that seemed to serve no useful purpose.

"Mr. Mullins," I called out.

"Adjusting course to intercept!" Mullins replied and *Revenge* altered her heading yet again.

"Devil take you," I muttered, scowling at the meandering schooner. "You're not right in the head."

"Are you talking to me?" Starkey asked. "Captain is a bloody lunatic."

"No." I cast a sharp glance his way. "Are you addressing me?"

"No, Captain, of course not..." Starkey smirked and wriggled his ears. He did that a lot, whether to laugh or lie. It was his tell, and also the reason he never won at cards.

"Don't get smart with me. I'll cut your ears off."

"Aye, Captain." Starkey threw back his head and laughed harder. His ears beat like wings.

Without fail, strumpets found the quirk endearing and clutched him to their bosoms, whereas elves perceived mockery and took offense. David, for his part, had no awareness or control over those twitchy things, so I herded him away from elves toward more amiable companionship. Fortunately, we had no faeries on board, so it wasn't often a problem. Nor was it ever likely to be. I distrust and dislike faerie folk; pixies and merfolk being the notable exceptions.

With a hearty harrumph, I returned my attention to the schooner, now floundering against the current. Her captain's sanity remained in question, but one thing was crystal clear: the schooner's skipper was grossly incompetent.

"Maybe I was mistaken," Starkey said out of the blue.

"About what?"

He shook his head. "That ship's origin..."

Irritation needled me. "How could you be mistaken? Were you so sloshed that you suffered the hallucination of a ship falling out of the sky?"

Revenge's crew consumed spirits while on duty and off, especially ale and diluted wine. The alcohol purified and improved the taste of the water. I understood this, the same as I *knew* Starkey hadn't been inebriated when he sighted the schooner. For one, I'd have smelled booze on his breath, but the truth of his character was even simpler than that. David never over-indulged enough to compromise his wits.

Starkey stiffened at the implicit insult. "I wasn't drunk and I know what I saw. It fell out of the sky."

My bark had a bite. "What are you saying then?"

He ducked his head. "I mean only that we live in a world full of faeries and magic. Strange and peculiar things happen all the time. Maybe this is due to something else. Maybe it's not Peter Pan..."

I tapped my foot. I understood what he was trying to do. By taking the blame, Starkey was deftly able to suggest that perhaps *I* had been wrong... Without actually saying so. The proposal annoyed me more than it should have, because I'd wondered the same thing myself—entertained the terrible self-doubt. A peculiar upset coalesced in my chest: the bitter taste of bile rose in the back of my throat.

"Don't be a dunce," I snapped. "It's Peter."

It had to be Pan because I *needed* for it to be Pan.

"Of course, Captain. I was stupid to think

otherwise." Starkey flattened his ears and lips together. Thereafter, the cat had his tongue.

We didn't speak of it again, but the conversation haunted me. Starkey was often flippant and always impulsive, but he was never stupid.... And I am often blinded by my obsession.

LESS THAN AN HOUR LATER, first light put any doubts to rest.

Dawn dribbled across the horizon, a gold and red smear—the broken yolk of a bloody egg. Morning heralded uneven, bucking surf. *Revenge* rocked, her decks rolled. I widened my stance for better stability.

Aboard the schooner, Peter Pan perched atop the railing of the sterncastle, a bright green splotch visible to the naked eye. Fury and loathing gathered like a storm, but I mastered and channeled the destructive energy.

Through the spyglass, I observed and performed a head count. Pan led a crew composed entirely of children. A lad of ten or so, clad in a nightcap and gown, manned the wheel. Three young boys clung to the rigging, but there was no sign of the delectable Tinker Bell.

Tink. The recollection of her delicate beauty struck me like a gut punch. A bitter brew of desire and distaste, anger and acrimony, flooded my soul. While the lovely faerie queen never dirtied her hands, she was complicit in the abduction and destruction of countless youths.

Revenge closed to a quarter mile.

"They still haven't seen us?" Starkey asked, sounding torn between amusement and disbelief.

"They have not." I clicked my tongue.

"That's an accomplishment." Starkey brought out his spyglass and aimed it at the schooner. After a delay, he said, "They don't appear to be ill."

"No, they do not." The visible lack of sickness gave me further cause for concern. The reason for the schooner's floundering state remained a mystery, and so I worried she might recover flight and escape.

Starkey snorted. "*Ariel.* Now there's a novel name."

"It suits her. That fine ship is meant to be a clipper. A shame she'd been kept from fulfilling her potential."

"She's not a clipper, Captain?" He looked askance at me.

"All sailors know three things make a clipper." I lowered the glass and savored the twist of irritation that crossed his face. The chit-chat provided a welcome distraction from the tension. "First, a clipper's lines are sharp and built for speed. Second, she's tall-sparred and carries the utmost spread of canvas."

"Aye, *Ariel's* all that." Starkey breathed out a wistful gust. He sounded far and away. That tone fanned the embers of my misgivings. An icy trickle of fear flowed through my veins.

I'd seen *that look* on a man's face before. John Rackham, my former second mate, had caught the fever of unrealized ambitions. He'd grown restless, and eventually he'd departed *Revenge* to pursue his goals. Now I suspected Starkey had the same yearning. He was daydreaming about capturing *Ariel*... and becoming her commander. Such ambition was unsurprising and perhaps inevitable... Sooner or later, all first mates entertained notions of ascending to captaincy.

Whether Starkey meant to step over my corpse to get there... that was the thing to watch out for. And the moment the unworthy thought crossed my mind, I sickened with shame. Paranoia was an ugly thing.

As a distraction, I crafted an impulsive diversion and asked, "Do you know what's keeping her from being a clipper, David? The thing that's lacking?"

Starkey jerked his face toward me. His cat's pupils dilated and he stared with unblinking regard. After a pondering delay, he said, "No, I don't."

I studied *Ariel*'s lines through the spyglass. "A vessel worthy of being named a clipper must use her sails, day and night, fair weather and foul."

He swallowed. "You're saying a ship's captain 'n' crew are every bit as important as the vessel herself."

"That's exactly what I mean."

"Aye," Starkey rolled out the lusty note. "You're right. But she *could* be a clipper."

"*Ariel*'s a pretty ship, I'll grant you. She's not a pirate captain's vessel, Starkey," I said, taking a harsher tone than was warranted.

Starkey cocked his head and stared. "I know."

You deserve better. I thought it but didn't say the words. I should have. With absolute and utter certainty, I knew Starkey would make an excellent master and commander.

"You can't blame a man for dreaming..." Starkey bared his teeth. A second later, he narrowed his eyes.

I expected him to ask, "*Can you?*"

He didn't and so I stayed damnably silent. For the official record... No. I never begrudged David his dreams, only feared losing my trusted first mate and friend.

I'd have given him a hand up...

If only he'd asked.

The moment passed. Uneasy in my own skin, I submersed myself in aggression. *Revenge* was almost within boarding distance. "Starkey, relieve Mr. Mullins. I want a deft navigator at the helm when we come alongside the schooner."

"You think I'm deft? Why, thank you!" Starkey preened.

Amusement bubbled through me, but I remained stern. "Mr. Mullins and twenty men of his choosing will accompany me when we board."

"Only twenty?" Starkey crushed his lips together.

"It's a ship of children, Starkey. The cabin boys should be able to take that vessel armed with wooden swords."

"And Pan?"

"Pan is mine." I thrust my hook overhead. The blue steel captured and reflected the sunlight. I'd cut down anyone stupid enough to get in my way.

"Now stop catching flies. I gave you orders. Get to it!"

"Aye!" Starkey saluted and then a rooster crowed.

"Cock-a-doodle-doo! Cock-a-doodle-doo!"

CHAPTER 5

Cock-a-Doodle-Doo!

"That bloody sound." I cringed, ducking my head, and clenched my fists. The piercing cry crawled across my skin like the hundred legs of a centipede.

"Took long enough," Starkey muttered, hunching his shoulders. He and I had our ears plugged, along with the rest of the crew, but Pan's summons still wrought a visible reaction from the first mate.

Pan waved his arms about and aimed the pointy tips of his slippers at the sky. All the while, he kept at that incessant, maddening cawing. "Cock-a-doodle-doo! Cock-a-doodle-doo!"

Pandemonium erupted on the schooner. Small figures poured onto the deck, running this way and that, their hands in the air. A predator sensing fear, *Revenge* awoke, but in a calm and disciplined fashion. My crew labored at their assigned tasks.

The infernal wretch continued without the slightest regard for his crew's full-blown panic. "Cock-a-doodle-doo! Cock-a-doodle-doo!"

"I'd give anything to shut him up," Starkey grated. "I wish I'd done it years ago when I had the chance. You don't know how I've regretted." The sharpness of his delivery had my attention, but one glance at his face reminded me. Starkey hated Peter Pan almost as much as I did—our mutual hatred of the fae king was one of the things that bound us together.

"You and me both."

"This time we end it." He bared his teeth in a tiger smile meant for me and me alone. We traded a knowing look. Visceral excitement flared between us. He and I both loved these adventures more than either of us would ever admit.

"This time." I returned his feral grin and the promise that bound us.

Starkey snapped off a smart salute and pounced. The leap carried him high into the air and to the sterncastle deck. He relieved Mr. Mullins at the helm and passed along the orders I'd given. Orders, like other things, roll downhill. *Revenge* bustled with focused energy and activity. She plowed steadily through the waves, closing on five hundred yards.

Through the spyglass, I located Pan's lithe green form again, but he didn't stay still for long. He bounded across the deck, making it a challenge to follow him. Pan waved his arms about and shouted haphazard orders such as "Swing the boom!" and "Adjust your rudder!"

On *Ariel*, a tragic comedy played out. The inexperienced crew jumped to obey, though their desperate bumbling left the ship dead in the water. The rudder turned one way—the boom swung in opposition. The wind pushed the pretty little ship like a slow-spinning top. Despite their vulnerability, worry ate at me. I feared Pan would execute a miraculous recovery. Should he restore his crew's morale, *Ariel* would recover flight and the schooner might escape into the clouds.

The gap narrowed to three hundred yards. So close, I could taste it. I was convinced Peter's day of reckoning had finally arrived. There would be no evasion or escape. My presence anchored Pan to this vast, lonely stretch of ocean and this confrontation. Hatred bound us, he and I, the gravity that kept pulling us together. Pan couldn't escape. *This time* I had him.

Dead to rights.

"Pan. You're finally going to get yours..." The nearer we drew, the tenser I grew. The wait was maddening. The sinew drew taut across my bones, and I wondered what would break first: my mind or body.

"Orders, Captain?" Starkey called.

"Hard to port!"

"Coming port!" Starkey sang out, and the ship turned, adopting a course that would take it parallel to *Ariel*.

Our sails tacked, and *Revenge* sliced through the sea. The crew heaved to, hard at work. On the main deck, the boarding party had gathered along the railing. They were armed with nets and boarding pikes as well as, grappling hooks and gangplanks. Soon, it'd be time for me to join them and lead the raid.

"Make your course one-four-eight."

"One-four-eight! Two hundred yards!"

"Steady as you go!"

"Steady as she goes!"

I had him now.

An Aurora Borealis of sparkles streaked across

Ariel's deck. Ah, at last. The delicious Tinker Bell made her glorious entrance. She flitted to and fro, trailing pixie dust in her wake. Agitation marked her flight, tight spikes and crimson sparkles.

On *Ariel,* panicked children scurried about like mice. Poor things, they wailed, sobbed, and fled, even though there was nowhere to go. Tinker Bell alone retained the aspect of rationality. She darted around the schooner, releasing a shower of pixie dust. If not for the lack of happy children, *Ariel* would've kited into the wind. The hullabaloo presented an opportunity to be taken advantage of before it passed.

Peter Pan floated above his frantic subjects. The eternal boy personified sullenness. His cap sat askew, and he crossed his arms over his chest, raining down commands to those below.

Magic imbued Pan's call to arms with resonance which exceeded the mundane. Even with my ears plugged with wax and my partial deafness to protect me, I *felt* it in my bones. "Stop running! We must gather together around the main mast to defend the ship! Be prepared to die for honor and glory!"

Some of the Lost Boys answered Pan's summons. They rallied, hurrying toward the main mast. Even the strongest-willed adults found Peter's voice difficult to resist. You can imagine how easily children succumbed to his sway. The development concerned me. An orderly defense made capturing the children without bloodshed more difficult.

Tinker Bell's appearance upped the stakes. My back and limbs ached under the burden of the strain, and I felt like I was about to break. Aggression surged through me, rendering clarity almost impossible. All I knew was that Pan must not be allowed to escape with those youngsters. The solution came to me as an epiphany: as a natural consequence, frightened children were unhappy children.

To that end, I raised my voice and shouted, "Run up the Red!"

At the helm, Starkey released the wheel and whirled to face aft. Wide-eyed, he looked to me for confirmation and mouthed, "The Red?"

"The Red!"

Our gazes locked. Starkey stared into my soul, understandably reluctant to implement such a drastic measure against a ship of children. I had a reputation for ruthlessness, but this crossed lines, even for the dread Captain Hook. Across the distance, I bore into him and brought my full force of will to bear.

I signed, "Obey your captain."

Starkey swallowed convulsively and nodded. He seconded the order to the pensive crew. "Run up the Red!"

Revenge's crew received the command with the wariness usually reserved for news of bad tidings. I'd already ordered the artillery readied. Their doubts were reasonable, especially given the circumstances.

In contrast, the Red—a flag with the visage of death on a scarlet field—was the standard of murderers. Its message: attack without mercy, no quarter given.

My crew obeyed, but they didn't want to. Dissension played out across the ship, muttered discussions and veiled glares aimed at their captain. They despised the order, but feared me too much to challenge my authority without a leader. Only Starkey and Smee possessed the backbone to even try. I had David's support—and Smee was confined to the infirmary.

We lowered the Black and ran up the Red. The red skull-and-crossbones flag whipped in the wind: it promised a violent and bloody death—no man, woman, *or child* spared.

"Open the gun ports!" I commanded.

The grates on the gun ports smashed open, a

resounding ruckus that rolled like thunder across the Neverland Sea. *Revenge* bristled with the muzzles of her deadly artillery, the majority located on the orlop deck above the waterline, now revealed. A merciless predator, she bore down on that hapless schooner.

Children screamed in terror.

CHAPTER 6

Boarding Parties—Tootles—The Elusive Nature
of Joy

The time had come to join the boarding party so I descended the sterncastle, heading forward. During the trip, I lost sight of Pan and Tinker Bell. The lapse troubled me, but other necessities demanded my attention. It would only be for a short time—a cold comfort—but it was the self-assurance I clung to and repeated.

Upon reaching the main deck, I met up with Mr. Mullins and the other men and women who composed the boarding party, a complement of veteran mariners, all of whom had served under me for years.

Revenge closed to seventy yards under Starkey's nimble navigation.

In the grip of churning impatience, I pressed against the starboard balustrade while the distance separating the ships shortened. The process seemed to take forever, an eternity of torture. It required the entirety of my willpower not to take a running leap at *Ariel* where the disorder had given way to pure chaos.

"Stick to your training!" I ordered the boarding party. "The goal is to subdue and restrain those children. As soon as you secure a captive, return to the ship. Prisoners are to be delivered to Dr. Chopp in the infirmary. Mr. Mullins, are the grapnels ready?"

"Aye, Captain!" Mr. Mullins held one of the iron grappling hooks aloft in a demonstration. Along the railing, four sailors followed his example, hoisting the fluked anchors with attached lines. Behind them, others maneuvered the footbridges into position.

The ships pulled broadside—twenty feet to go.

"Stand ready!" In those final seconds, my heart stroked like a hammer on an anvil. The second the ships came into position, I gave the order. "Now! Throw the grapnels!"

"Hurrah!" The boarding party bellowed with hearty enthusiasm, and they sprang into smooth, coordinated action.

Grappling hooks soared through the air, descended on the schooner's deck, and latched onto her railings. Once the hooks grabbed hold, the pirates assigned to the boarding parties took up the slack. The lines grew taut. *Revenge* hauled her prey closer, a tigress with her claws sunk in a helpless gazelle.

Bursting with impatience, I leaned out and watched for my enemy. The paranoid voice in the back of my head would not be silenced until I located Pan again and confirmed he hadn't escaped. For a frustrating moment, the search came up empty, but then I spotted Peter in the shadow of *Ariel's* main mast, hiding behind the line of Lost Boys that'd rallied to his defense.

Tinker Bell hovered eye level with Pan, and anger transformed her golden blonde tresses to fiery red. The faerie queen wore a gown of flames and her pixie aura billowed with smoldering cinders and ash. They appeared to be arguing.

"What's this? Trouble in paradise?" I asked with a snide snicker. I was torn between curiosity and malicious delight. Naturally, I wondered what their row was about. Peter faced away from me so I couldn't see what he was saying. Instead, I focused on Tinker Bell. I read her perfect bow lips, as enticing as a kiss.

Tinker Bell said to Peter, "How dare you blame me? The ship won't fly because of her! This is all HER fault!"

My heart stopped. For a second, I couldn't think or breathe. I assumed Tinker Bell meant *me*. The accusation evoked a bizarre, paralyzing quagmire of guilt and shame. The squall blew over, but not before the damage had been done. It penetrated my defenses. I shook from head to toe, and to stop quaking, I stiffened until the sinew in my limbs threatened to snap.

The momentary weakness lasted seconds, but it had cost me. I'd missed whatever Tink had said next. The cause of their conflict would remain a mystery. Just as I looked up, a slender figure with tousled chestnut tresses, clad in a flowing periwinkle nightgown, dashed across Ariel's deck and ran up to Peter.

My heart stopped, and my breath hissed through my teeth. I prayed for the youth to be a longhaired boy. Of course, there was no god listening, and certainly not one that would answer the petition of the despicable likes of me. The child turned her head and I got a clear look at her face. My hopes dashed against a sorrowful sea.

A storm of rage consumed me whole. I breathed fire. "Pan's got a girl on board. *A girl!*"

Those closest to me cringed and drew away. I *felt* rather than heard Starkey shouting my name, but I ignored him. My fury was unstoppable.

Dragged like a toy on a rope, the schooner's port side smashed against our starboard. The collision rocked both ships, but *Ariel*, having less mass, bore the brunt of it. Once the worst of the swaying passed, the crew tied down the five grappling lines, leaving a gap of about twenty feet. It almost killed me, but I held the order to board until the moorings were secured and the vessels bound together.

"On my word!" I thrust my hook skyward. The sunlight flashed off steel.

"Hurrah!" The crew rallied, roaring with blood lust. They heaved three footbridges straight up, ready to be dropped into position.

"Lower the gangplanks!" I shouted and the timbers fell. The three footbridges rested on the railings, descending from *Revenge* to the schooner, forming pathways across the water.

A roar tore from my throat. Leading the charge, I stepped first on the nearest footbridge, sprinted down the ramp, and sprang onto the main deck. I landed in a crouch, the leads of the hunting net dangling from my fingers, and surged forward to make way for those boarding behind me. The others followed right on my heels, hitting the planks with resounding thuds that moved through my center like the pulsating beats of a drum.

About a dozen scruffy Lost Boys who'd found the courage to fight rather than run gathered about the main mast, standing with their backs to the post in a tight defensive circle. They'd armed themselves with whatever they could find; a few had knives and others clubs. Like a coward, Pan soared into the air, holding the girl's hand. They ascended together. I didn't understand whether she flew on her own or he dragged her, and there wasn't time to decide.

"Spread out! Let's round them up," I ordered, and those already on deck took up positions to either side of me.

To the rear of the company, Mr. Mullins repeated the command, "You heard the captain! Byron, flank to the bow! Keats, to the stern!"

We welded into a unified front and advanced on the armed boys. All around us, Lost Boys launched themselves at my crew with the fervor of Viking raiders. Pan inspired unnerving fervor in his mesmerized followers.

My attention ought to have been focused entirely on what stood before me, but an irresistible compulsion forced my gaze upward to where Pan hung in the air. His detachment nettled my skin, causing hot, itchy prickles to spread like a rash. I fully expected him to swoop down to engage the pirates boarding his ship—to fight *me*. In the past, the brash, overconfident braggart had always leapt straight into the fray. So why wasn't he now? It was, in a word, an aberration.

Motion in the periphery of my vision caught my attention. Riding a surge of excitement, I snapped to attention and brought my hook up to parry. A rotund boy of perhaps ten years of age leapt into my path.

Sweat shone on his brow, and he struggled to lift a rusty cutlass that was obviously too heavy. With a grunt, he hauled the blade in an overhand swing aimed at my knee.

"I'm rather fond of that particular appendage," I said and sidestepped. "It's one of the three I have left."

The boy huffed and puffed out his plump

cheeks. He wound up for another assault. "Die, you scurrilous pirate!"

"Is that a slur or a bold statement of the obvious?"

"Prepare to feel the wrath of Tootles the Wolf!" He stabbed and I evaded.

"A wolf, are you? I mistook you for a polecat." I cocked my head, studying young Tootles. He wore an ill-fitted costume of what I judged to be raccoon skins that were sloppily sewn together, and—from the rank stench—improperly cured. I simply couldn't see a wolf, but I did try.

Tootles lobbed the cutlass my way again. "You'll die for that insult!"

This time, I parried his blade with my hook. The metal weapons clanked together, steel scraping against steel. "Well then, speak well of how bravely I fought and well I died when you tell the tale of the day you bested Captain Hook."

"Liar! You're a liar, you are! Captain Hook is a man and Peter Pan killed him!" the boy proclaimed with great bluster. *Oh, by Jove!* The very suggestion that the notorious pirate foe of Peter Pan might be a woman had reduced the lad to sputtering outrage.

A vein throbbed in my temple. My brain threatened to explode. *This again.* For years, Pan had persisted in spreading the rumor that Captain Hook was male, though his exact motives remained a mystery. Maybe he wished to vex me, or perhaps he simply preferred his twisted version because it made for a better story.

"Pan lied," I bit off. Tootles opened his mouth to reply, but I'd hear none of it. My patience had reached its end. With a twist of my wrist, I forced the blade from his hand and sent it flying.

Tootles paled in terror, then threw up his hands and backed away. With an expert flip, I tossed the hunting net over him. The weighted leads wrapped around the boy, entangling him. Without breaking stride, I swooped, caught the writhing child up in my arms, and swept him off his feet. He reeked of urine and rotted hides, and I gagged at the smell. I tucked the kicking boy beneath my arm and turned on my heel. Mr. Byron was the first man I encountered. He had empty arms, so I handed over my captive.

"Mr. Byron, take this child to Smee. See to it he receives a bath and a fresh set of clothing." I might've mentioned a proper meal, but the hefty lad clearly wasn't suffering for lack of nourishment. If anything, he wanted for moderation and exercise.

"Aye, Captain!" Byron tossed the boy over his shoulder and returned to the nearest footbridge.

Several members of the boarding party who'd also taken prisoners were crossing to *Revenge*.

I turned to assess the condition on *Ariel's* main deck. The boarding party had the situation well under control. More than half the Lost Boys were disarmed and subdued, and the others would soon be also. Having satisfied my concern, I turned my attention outward and upward.

Tinker Bell streaked past, running the starboard balustrade like a track. Glimmer trailed in her wake. If she'd come closer, I might've doffed my hat and taken a swipe at capturing her, but she stayed out of reach. I twisted around to look up at Pan, who balanced on tippy toe on the main sail rigging.

The girl with the chestnut curls in the periwinkle nightgown floated alongside him. She was a pretty chit, but something of a doll with her unfocused gaze and blank expression. He gripped her hand, tethering her like a buoyant kite eager to fly off. A growl of pure frustration ripped from my throat, because the precarious nature of her plight was not lost on me. A fall from that height would surely kill her.

"Pan! Face me!" I shouted so hard my throat ached. Determined to force his attention, I shook my hook, the standard under which my crew united and fought.

Peter glanced down. A frown pinched his elf-fair features. He appeared thoroughly discombobulated. And there, I was left wondering if the king of pretenders remembered me not at all. Was that not a truly tragic thing—to be erased from history? To my way of thinking, an individual enjoyed a sort of enduring immortality so long as others spoke their name. The soul lived on in infamy. Having one's name forgotten was the worst fate imaginable.

"Who are you?" Pan asked, and from the slackness in his face, I *knew* he wasn't lying. Aye, he'd expunged the memory of Captain Hook from his twisted psyche.

The insult enraged me. My blood *burned*.

"I am Captain Jayden Hook," I sneered in the grip of fervor. Bitterness twisted in my chest. I'd have loved nothing more than to put all thoughts of Peter Pan from my head forever. Why should he enjoy the luxury I never could?

"Hook. Captain Hook?" Peter frowned and mouthed my name over and over. His head flopped over like the head of a cut blossom aged past its freshness. Seconds drained away. Peter's face twisted and turned. For a split second, his mask cracked, revealing the wicked soul that lurked beneath his facade of innocence. To blink would've been to miss it.

I whispered encouragement, "There you go. You remember me now."

Recognition and then hatred flared in Peter's gaze. He pointed and cried, "Captain Hook! Fiend!"

I returned his glare, a thorn for a thorn, and brandished my hook, aimed at his heart. "I'm coming for you."

Pan caught my gaze and curled his upper lip in a sneer of pure disdain. Salt in the wound, he stuck out his tongue. *Let him.* I'd rip it out by the root.

"If you won't descend, I'll come after you." I headed for the main mast, intending to climb the ladder. I'd damn well fight him in the rigging—I feared neither heights nor falling.

Before I reached the post, however, Peter screeched at a pitch that split hairs and frayed nerves. "Think happy thoughts! Think happy thoughts!"

I could've been cold-stone deaf in both ears, and still I'd have heard him. Dead calm fell across *Ariel*; all motion ceased. A hush fell. It affected me, too. The foul faerie magic penetrated my core and turned me inside out.

My steps faltered. My boots rooted themselves to the deck.

"Think happy thoughts! Think happy thoughts!" Pan crowed his dominating message—drove the command into my head until it consumed me.

Happiness... such an elusive, yet tantalizing concept, full of mystery and promise. Never had I experienced pure, unadulterated joy. I wanted it. *Needed it.* I reached for elation, but without anything more than an abstract understanding of what it was I strove to attain. The present offered no inspiration. At times, I enjoyed a fragile sense of contentment at best. I faced a future without optimism. Naught but a glum and dark destiny awaited me, and the most I hoped for was a quick and painless death. In desperation, I turned to the past, which held brief moments, sparks of cheer. Those lazy afternoons spent with Starkey on Blackberry Bluff... My life was devoid of intimacy and connection. Nothing, absolutely nothing, rivaled my abhorrence of Peter Pan.

Leaden hatred anchored me to misery.

An electrifying current passed through *Ariel.* My feet tingled under the assault of hundreds of pleasurable pricks. All of a sudden, heat surged through me, my heart raced, and I was breathing hard.

"All your thoughts are happy," Pan chanted.

The ship trembled. Lost Boys and pirates alike were trapped like living statues, stuck in their final positions. Despite their plugged ears, the boarding party had still fallen prey to Peter's spell... Since our last encounter, his power had grown substantially.

Alarm blazed through me. I might be a failure at happiness, but command was the blood in my veins. Concern for the craft and crew penetrated my pathetic contemplation of bliss. My gut feeling warned that my people were in danger, but when I tried to turn around, my body refused to obey. Frustration rampaged through me. I marshalled raw willpower. Like a bull, I snorted and stomped the planks, fighting to force my heavy limbs to obey. Anger became my armor and the vigor that drove me. One stumbling step led to another. I channeled all my strength into the effort, gathering momentum.

"You're so happy, you're lighter than air!" Pan's song assaulted my mind, the sharp sting of hailstones. He led a chorus with the others repeating every lyric, and his power grew.

A halo of shimmering radiance enveloped the schooner. Pixie dust... it defied description. The most eloquent poet couldn't do its beauty justice. The sight of it imbued a breathless sense of wonder and emboldened the imagination. It was erratic, ephemeral, and ethereal... By daylight, it was a fizzy rainbow. Under moonlight, it glowed opalescent. It held the essence of joy, beauty beyond the stars in the sky.

Ariel pitched and lifted skyward.

CHAPTER 7

Airships—Melodrama—BOOM

"All hands, abandon ship!" A yell burst from my throat and I erupted into action. I seized hold of my crewmembers' shoulders and shook them. They flopped like rag dolls. I shouted at the top of my lungs, trying to drown out Pan's voice and break the enchantment, but they remained zombies.

Fever burned through me, but a persistent thought sprang into the back of my mind—what was Starkey doing? Surely he had seen what was happening to the boarding party. Or had the thing I dreaded the most come true—had *Revenge's* crew also succumbed to Pan's bewitchment?

"Come to your senses!" I tore across the deck, shoving my crew. By chance, I came upon Mr. Keats. When I barked orders full in his face, he only returned a blank stare. I slapped him... nothing.

The ship lifted a couple feet, and the footbridges dislodged from the balustrades. The tumbled gangplanks took a few of my people with them. The startled yelps of plunging pirates split the air.

Inspiration struck. I dragged Mr. Keats to the railing and shoved him over the side. If falling didn't wake him up, then the cold dunking would. *Ariel* floated a good ten feet over the ocean now. I reached out, making a blind grab, and latched onto another member of my crew. Beaver followed Mr. Keats into the Neverland Sea.

Ariel continued her ascent. The grappling lines, those five braided hemp ropes, drew taut. The schooner tilted to her port side. Hapless children and passive pirates slid across the deck and smashed into the railing. The moorings bought us a little more time, and another half dozen of my people joined Beaver and Keats in the water. I refrained from tossing any youngsters overboard, however. Every member of my crew could swim, but I didn't know about the minors.

Breathing hard, I spared precious seconds and surveyed *Revenge*. The stolen glance confirmed the worst of my fear—the crewmembers in my line of sight were living statues. I searched, but couldn't find Starkey.

Off *Ariel's* port side, a green figure streaked through the sky. *Peter Pan*. My gut clenched. I hauled the sailor in my grip over the side and grabbed hold of the railing to secure my balance.

Pan sliced the first line and the schooner rolled. In rapid succession, smaller shudders rocked the vessel as two successive ropes were severed. Crowing like a damnable rooster, Peter flew toward the fourth mooring, which was closest to me.

A baldric holding three flintlock pistols was draped across my chest. I drew a gun and fired without taking aim. The muzzle belched sparks and sulfurous smoke.

The shot missed.

Peter cut the fourth line and flew for the final mooring.

I dropped the empty weapon to the deck. Riding a reckless surge, I yanked the second pistol and took the shot.

Missed again.

"Blast you!" I cursed Pan.

The third pistol cracked, spewing a flash of brimstone. Three times in a row, the bullet failed to find its mark. A shout tore from my throat, and I may well have stomped out my frustration. Any other time—*any other time*—I was an excellent marksman. But when it mattered, I couldn't hit the broadside of a ship.

Peter cut the remaining grappling line, and *Ariel* resumed her ascent, once again rising heavenward.

I shoved the remaining pistol into my belt and tossed two more of *Revenge's* crew into the sea. The exertion had begun to take its toll. My muscles burned, and I labored for breath. Despite my determined effort, about half the raiding party remained on board. Soon, we'd be too high for anyone to make a safe jump. Once the ship soared into the clouds, Pan would certainly compel anyone who was left to leap to their deaths. I needed to think of something and fast.

Starkey, where are you? Damn it, I need you.

In the grip of powerful frustration, I whirled and immediately slammed to a halt. Tinker Bell hovered before me in her full five-and-a-half-inch glory. Panting hard, I stared at her... she gawked at me. We gaped at each other, but upon doing so we were every bit as fascinated as a mongoose and a cobra.

Tink's succulent lips rounded into a pretty O, revealing the pinkness of her tongue just past the part. Golden-blonde tresses fell to her shoulders in a cascade, and she wore a light blue frock too tight and too short to contain her ample curves. Blimey, but she was a peach... a ripe, succulent peach just begging for a full bite. Tooth and tongue. My mouth watered for her sweetness.

"Get off the ship, Hook, before it's too late." Tinker Bell joined her hands together, pleading for me to obey.

"Not without my crew."

"Please, Peter will kill you."

"That would be nothing new. I've made a bargain with the Grim Reaper. I'll bow willingly before her scythe, but only after Pan has died by my hand."

Tinker Bell rolled her eyes. "Oh, Hook, always so dramatic."

Intent on murder, I tilted my head back. Pan perched in the rigging—the rooster on his roost—where I expected him to be. The passive girl was still with him.

Peter smirked and loosened his grip so he

supported her with two fingers. He crooked his hand and mouthed, "Come here now or I'll let her go."

My heart surged and thudded against my chest. Icy fear gripped me. Hefting my hook, I advanced a stride toward the main mast. "I'll eviscerate you gullet to groin!"

Tinker Bell darted into my path. "Hook, what about your crew?"

"They'll be safe once Pan's dead. Step aside, love. I don't wish to harm you." Abruptly, a chilling sense of wrongness crashed over me again. My skin crawled. None of the day's events made even a lick of sense. Not Pan's Machiavellian scheming or Tinker Bell's sudden interest in dissuading me from my most driving goal. If anyone should grasp the futility of trying to talk me out of revenge, it was Tinker Bell.

"You don't understand. *Pan's different.*"

Different how? It begged the question. Under less pressing circumstances, I'd have been delighted to indulge Tink's games, but now I had neither the time nor the inclination. My crew, the children, and the girl needed saving.

Pan had to be slain.

"Step aside." This time, I didn't wait for her refusal. I lunged, wrapped my hand around Tinker

Bell's waist, and swung her aside. The faerie queen was a featherweight.

On reaching the main mast, I climbed the ladder hand over hook. While I ascended, Peter Pan retreated higher with the impassive girl in tow. His uncharacteristic retreat baffled and irritated me from the get-go. Pan was many things, but not craven. I wondered if this was the "difference" Tinker Bell had mentioned.

The higher *Ariel* ascended, the harder the wind whipped. The ocean receded to a slate-blue field far below. I could only guess at our altitude, but it must've been at least a hundred feet by the time I reached the top.

Standing on the platform, I drew my cutlass. A duel in the rigging would require strength and dexterity, and I was already weary. Concern for the girl made me cautious. Taunting Pan into approaching me was the best bet, but would he fall for it?

"Fight me, Peter. Or are you too fearful?"

"I'm not afraid of you, Hook! The opposite. You and your pathetic obsession... you're not worth the effort." Pan kicked off the mast and floated between the shrouds, still holding the girl's hand. He brandished his enchanted knife, the same blade he'd used to sever the grappling lines.

I got my first clear view of Pan since this whole thing had started. Tinker Bell had been telling the truth. The eternal boy *looked* different somehow, although exactly what had altered eluded me. I scowled, trying to sort it out. Insight came to me in an epiphany. As long as I'd known Peter Pan, he'd appeared to be a beautiful boy of eight or nine. Now, I placed him at ten years old. He'd grown longer in the limbs, and his face had lost that cherubic shine. The change confounded me.

An astonished outburst escaped me in a great gust. "You've aged!"

"Liar! You're a filthy, dastardly, dishonest pirate!" Pan aimed the point of his knife at my throat and waved his other arm in a thoughtless gesture, causing the poor girl to shake. Worry pricked me. What if Peter forgot he was the only thing keeping her aloft?

"Slander! I'm imminently clean. You're a blundering fool." I wanted to engage him further, to attempt to provoke him into revealing more, but the girl took priority. Less than fifty feet separated us; it may as well have been miles. I cast a fast glance around, surveying my options. The flintlock pistol only fired one shot, which I'd already used. Even if

I'd brought additional firearms, I couldn't have risked hitting the girl.

"If you want to fight, then come to me! Or are you too *chicken?*" Pan sneered with a poorly contrived cunning. Clearly, his clever ploy was meant to lure me into the perilous rigging. Perhaps if he understood I had already decided to do just that, he would've come up with a better gibe.

"You're the damn rooster." I snagged a shroud with my hook and cut the base of the line from where it attached to the platform. Then, I returned the cutlass to its sheath and grasped the dangling rope. It required a couple precious seconds to gauge distances and angles.

I kicked off, swinging out in a wide arc.

Far below, thunder boomed, a racket so deafening it obliterated the thoughts in my head. *Revenge* fired her starboard battery, spewing fire and smoke. The cannonballs passed harmlessly beneath the schooner and crashed into the ocean. *Revenge* had only discharged a few of her starboard guns, but it was enough. The roar should've shattered Pan's hypnotic hold on his victims.

Ariel plummeted. I more imagined than actually heard the startled cries that erupted from the children and my crew when the deck dropped out from beneath their feet.

Peter Pan, of course, defied gravity. The line in my hands slackened when the mast dropped, leaving me in freefall.

Excellent timing, Mr. Starkey.

CHAPTER 8

Falling—Blackout—Small Victories

The passage of time slowed to a crawl, just as it always did when events went to bedlam all at once. *Ariel* was a few hundred feet high. The schooner plunged seaward at the rate of molasses, a sticky and inevitable advance. It blazed like a shooting star: a brilliant pixie-dust aura engulfed the ship from her rigging to her keel, including the glowing rope in my grip. I suspected faerie magic was what slowed her descent—and mine. Regardless, the lapse granted precious seconds to ponder my options, weighing possible choices and consequences.

Falling was a lot like flying, except for the part where it ended abruptly. I clung to the glowing rope, and continued to swing in a wide arc. My plan was to hold on until the last possible second. Better to go with the flow than to risk getting tangled—and possibly hanged—in the rigging.

Revenge discharged another artillery round, this time off her port side, away from *Ariel*. The schooner struck the ocean with a great splash.

The line in my hands snapped. I let go and turned like an arrow into the flight. Everything sped up and flashed past, fragments in a blur. *Ariel's* balustrade rushed straight at me, filling my vision. I was falling too fast to avoid the collision so I threw out my arms to shield myself. Better broken bones than a cracked skull or snapped spine. I twisted, trying to alter my trajectory, but no such luck.

Blackness.

I came to consciousness slowly, floating through a formless void. My whole body ached, but especially my shoulder. It hurt to breathe. I groaned, and a flurry of bubbles streamed from my mouth, which at least answered the question of where I was —underwater. I had no idea how long I'd been submerged, breathing water and drifting without the faintest idea of what was up or down.

Fortunately, I'm an experienced diver. I've spent years of my life beneath the waves, so I understood the ocean—its mysterious movements and consuming passion.

By an act of will, I ceased struggling and surrendered, floating with my limbs relaxed and senses open. In a receptive state, I could perceive the telltale hints which pointed toward the surface. The weight of my hook dragged my arm down while my body's natural buoyancy pushed in the opposite direction. Sunshine filtered through the water, informing my sense of direction. I gathered myself, executed a smooth flip, and swam toward the light.

While I'd been out, the current had pulled me down deep. It took a full minute of swimming for all I was worth to reach topside. The moment my head broke the surface, I vomited water until my lungs cleared enough to once again draw air. Coughing wracked my chest and rendered me helpless. To add insult to injury, an opportunistic breaker slapped me in the face and I inhaled a draught of fluid that left me gagging.

In such moments, I must confess to being tempted to resume singing. Gills would've come in handy right then. What harm would there be in voicing the refrains necessary to nudge my physical transformation into merfolk along? Of course, I didn't—I mustn't. And so I was miserable as a result...

Every now and then, fate tossed me a bone. Once the spasm subsided and I could breathe well enough to see again, I turned my face heavenward. Being an accomplished pessimist, I fully expected to discover nothing to greet my gaze but sea and sky.

By now, I reckoned Starkey would've declared me dead 'n' gone. If he had a lick of sense, he'd claimed the captaincy—and *Revenge*. Any pirate worth his salt, myself included, would've done so without hesitation. The wind filling the sails of a fine ship—and total freedom—was every swashbuckler's dream. I wouldn't have begrudged him in the least.

So imagine my surprise when a dark shadow fell over my face. I blinked salt water from my eyes and stared up in wonder. The sun shone behind the vessel, presenting the silhouette of a tall ship. No details, but I'd recognize her profile anywhere. My beautiful *Revenge*; she was the loveliest sight I'd ever laid eyes on. She rocked on robust swells. I swam to her bow and placed my palm against her ebonized oak hull. I wept with joy, tears which the ocean then swallowed whole.

A strangled cry tore from my throat, a pitiful effort, too quiet to carry to the deck. I summoned the last of my reserves and released a bellow worthy of a wounded bear. This time, someone heard me. A figure gazed over the railing on the fo'c'sle, scanning the surf. I heaved my hook overhead and flagged him.

Upon spotting me, he shouted, "Man overboard!"

"Captain, you dunce!"

"Oi, it's the captain! Captain Hook overboard!"

The alert spread. A great ruckus aroused, the many voices joined together. The crew crowded onto the decks and a ladder was tossed down. I swam to it and grabbed hold. With the last of my strength, I hauled myself up the rungs. Once I reached the railing, helping hands seized my arms. They dragged me over and dumped me onto the deck, where I sprawled in a boneless heap on my back. Ah, but what a sodden, weary wretch I must've looked. In my aching misery, I didn't care a whit about dignity.

"Well, look what the cat dragged in!" Starkey stood over me with his hands on his hips. His grin stretched from ear to ear. The crew had a good and hearty guffaw, and I joined them. Under normal circumstances, I'd have put the fear of Hook into them, but I believe they were genuinely glad to have me back, and I was ecstatic to be home.

I raised my arm, reaching for Starkey. He caught hold of my hand and hauled me upright. Instead of letting go, however, he held on. Good thing, too, because I swayed like tall grass on a gusty day.

"What's our status?" I asked.

"The ship is undamaged. We had a few casualties among the boarding party who got knocked overboard or jumped. Broken bones 'n' fractured skulls, but no one died. You were the last one missing."

"Exactly how long was I gone?" I stepped away from Starkey, breaking his hold. I'd been on my feet long enough to have recovered somewhat. He let go, but his hands flapped in that nervous manner of mothers with toddlers taking their first steps.

"You were under water over an hour."

I hesitated because I loathed requesting bad news, but it had to be done. "What happened to Pan?"

Starkey scowled. "Pan got away. While we were fishing our people out of the water, Pan bewitched the children and got the schooner airborne again. The ship flew away. I'm sorry, Captain. I could've tried to stop him, but—"

"You chose correctly." I gripped his bicep. Without having to ask, I sensed the loss tasted bitter to him, too. *Revenge's* first mate reviled Pan almost as much as her captain.

"We captured six Lost Boys. Two of 'em are underfed. Another had a nasty cut on his toe that needed tending. But Mr. Smee was pleased as punch that none of the children are carrying the pox."

"What good fortune!" I forced false cheer, but my heart wasn't in it. Between the exhausting ordeal and my injuries, staying upright proved a challenge in and of itself.

Starkey's tiger ears were tightly pressed back. He spoke so quietly I had to read his lips to understand. "I saw you hit *Ariel's* side. It looked like you'd broken your neck, and I thought for sure I'd lost you..."

He swallowed convulsively.

I grasped his shoulder tightly. "You should be so lucky, my friend. You should be so lucky. "

After Dr. Chopp attended to my injuries, I adjourned to recuperate and nurse my wounded pride. The great cabin had long been my sanctuary. Now, *great cabin* had a grand and pretentious ring. It opened the imagination, conjuring images of a vast and lofty hall. Allow me to provide some dimensions to establish a sense of scale.

The great cabin spanned the width of the stern,

and was located beneath the navigation room and above the galley. Arched multi-paned windows overlooked the ocean. The entire level had once been the captain's quarters, but it'd been far more space than I required. I'd had an interior bulwark constructed along the beam, dividing the area into two separate, equal-sized rooms adjoined by a connecting door. My quarters were portside; the starboard chamber served as the library, conservatory, and officers' conference room. Crowded built-in bookshelves lined the interior walls. Dead center, there was a mahogany table cluttered with maps and logbooks, a brass compass, sextants, and drawing implements.

There, Mr. Brown joined me for a light supper of grilled swordfish with sautéed garlic and shallots in a white wine sauce. Virgil wore a cloak of sobriety. We dined in silence, trading only a few necessary words.

In a move that surprised me, Mr. Brown proposed a toast. "Here's to the good we accomplished today."

"What good? Pan got away." I scoffed from bitterness, but raised my glass anyway. The encounter with Peter constituted yet another defeat in a long, drawn-out war. At times like those, in the depths of depression, I wondered what deity I'd mortally offended. Was I cursed to endless and ruinous failure?

Virgil's hands were rock steady. Candlelight glittered off the uncut ruby in his pinky ring. "Ah, but we saved the lives—and arguably the souls—of six boys."

"I suppose." I granted him the point, but begrudgingly.

The glasses clinked and we drank. The burgundy was rich, but a tad too sweet. I appreciated his kindness, though: words which provided immeasurable comfort. Mr. Brown was right. Today's accomplishment had to count for something. Losing constantly was taking its toll on the crew's morale... and on my spirit.

We claimed our victories where we could.

CHAPTER 9

A Bit o' Geography—Rackham's Cay—The Smee
Home for Lost Boys

Neverland is the largest island in the archipelago known as the Neverlands, which is composed of many delightful isles born from children's dreams. Islands, by definition, are small bodies of land surrounded by water, thus one could reasonably extrapolate that the Neverlands exist in some distant, poorly explored corner of the world.

That would be wrong.

Contrary to good logic, the Neverlands are found in the night sky amid countless moons and stars.

Those heavenly bodies hold a character in common that is both bohemian and capricious. Upon occasion, a lunar body will simply change its mind about where it wishes to go and alter its course. It makes for tricky seas and sailing.

The fae call our world the Ever After, and the mundane home of men the Otherworld, or simply, the Other.

Time. It exists, but its passage is unpredictable. Clocks refuse to keep accurate count, so we depend on star charts and sundials. Once upon a time, an accurate time-teller existed, but the artifact had been lost, and become stuck in the belly of a crocodile... along with my left hand.

FOLLOWING the fateful encounter with Pan, *Revenge* set sail for Rackham's Cay, a bustling port and the home base of Captain John Rackham, a pirate of some repute who was also the governor of the township...

Once we weighed anchor, *Revenge* required restocking and minor repairs, but truth be told, her captain needed the recovery time more than the ship or crew. In the meanwhile, Mr. Smee offloaded our precious cargo and attended to seeing the children settled into their new residence, the Smee Home for Lost Boys. From there, the maternal Mrs. Eleanora Smee took those misguided youths under her maternal wing and assumed responsibility for their well-being and tutelage.

The newest additions brought the number of boys under her care to thirteen. Someday, I intended to return the Lost Boys to their parents and families, though thus far my ambitions had proven nothing more than a pipe dream. I had never found the means to escape the Neverlands. The failure haunted me. The rescued children lived, however, and that served as some consolation.

Better orphans than corpses, eh?

CHAPTER 10

Return to Neverland—A Quest of Trust

We spent ten days in port. On the eleventh, we departed Rackham's Cay for Neverland. The return voyage took twice as long as the trip out because of an inclement headwind and shifting tides. Our course brought us into the Devil's Deep, the waters northeast of Neverland. We dropped anchor at a favored haunt, the formidable bulk of Devil's Rock between the ship and the mainland. The position provided concealment and ready access to the eastern end of the island.

During our sojourn, I'd devised a plan for

rescuing the girl in the periwinkle frock and plucking *Ariel* from Pan's grasp. But first, both must be located, which meant going ashore. To that end, I had the dinghy readied.

Amidst the hustle and bustle, Starkey followed me into my quarters. While I packed, he argued against my plan, forcing me to close the cabin door to ensure our privacy. When a first mate and captain disagreed, it incited the crew to unrest. For the umpteenth time, he asked, "Why can't I come with you?"

A heavy sigh hissed past my lips. I took a break from packing and straightened. By now, Starkey had made it clear he wouldn't simply let the matter go. "You're the first mate and I'm the captain. When I go ashore, it's your job to remain on the ship. I only anticipate being gone a day, but if it takes longer, I need for you to ensure a bunch of restless fools don't stage a mutiny and sail off with my vessel."

"And if something happens to you?"

"Then *Revenge* is yours, and I'll die knowing she's in good hands."

Starkey clearly disliked the compliment. He worked his jaws and jutted out his chin, adopting a stubborn pose that bore a striking resemblance to the thirteen-year-old tiger-boy I'd first met so many years ago.

"I want to go with you," he said.

"Duty and desire seldom intersect."

"You could use my help. I know Neverland better than you. I lived here longer." *Truth—the isle had almost turned him into a tiger.*

"Maybe so, but you're needed here. Even with my limited capacity, I imagine I can find my way around the isle to get where I'm going," I said through clenched teeth, because I was ill disposed to repetition. The onset of a headache throbbed in my temples. There were two members of the crew I'd tolerate such a blatant challenge from: Smee, who I needed, and Starkey, my oldest and dearest companion.

"Mullins can manage the ship for a day. *If,*" Starkey had sarcasm rife in his tone, "it'll really be that quick."

"Mr. Mullins is a competent second mate, but I don't trust him—"

"But you trust me?" Starkey growled low in his throat. He leveled a glare, bared his fangs, and brought his fists up.

The muscles in my face hardened. The taunt thrust straight past my guard and struck its target.

Needle-thin cold lanced my heart. Of late, I'd questioned Starkey's loyalty, but only in the privacy of my own thoughts. Up until that moment, I believed I'd kept my doubts hidden from him. Obviously, I was mistaken. That familiarity he and I shared, it went both ways, a fact I must never forget.

"I trust you."

Starkey sneered. "Are you sure about that? I've seen the distrust in your eyes. It started the day we first sighted *Ariel* and I admitted to admiring her. For the sin of looking at another ship, I've become a suspected traitor."

I almost swallowed my tongue and choked. A coughing spell ensued before I managed to clear my throat. "That's absurd."

"Is it?"

"Absolutely," I said, lying through my teeth. Paranoia... she was such a twisted, lovely creature. She had me jumping through hoops, treating my faithful first mate—and best friend—with mistrust.

In all honesty, I'd been holding Starkey at a distance with both arms, but not for the reasons he thought. The truth was far uglier...and pettier... than concerns of backstabbing and mutiny. Selfishness had sunk its claws in deep. The specter of Starkey leaving—just as John had done—haunted me.

I needed David.

Starkey wasn't having any of it. "You know, I've been wondering what it'd mean to have my own ship. Can I be my own man while I'm living in your shadow?"

"You can't flourish under a woman's command?" My tone grew churlish. Starkey was the last man I'd expected to spout sexist rhetoric.

"What? No!" Starkey sneered, then scoffed. "You're no woman!"

"I'm not? Malarkey!" My eyebrows tried to leap clean off my face. I wondered if he spoke in jest, but Starkey's ears gave not the slightest tremor.

"Don't go making this about that. It's *never* been about that."

"Do you have a point, man? Or do you aim to win this dispute by confounding me speechless?"

"My point is this! Either you trust me, or you don't. I'm sick to death of your hooded gazes and long silences. If you don't, after all these years, then I might as well call it quits. Maybe I'll take *Revenge* out for a joy ride while you're away!" He pounded his fist into his palm.

Explosive tension permeated the air, Starkey and I locked together in an unwavering standoff. The lit fuse on the bomb burned down, releasing its bitter, ashy fumes. Comradeship drew us together while stress tore us apart.

"Is that your plan?" I asked.

David blinked. "What?"

"Are you planning on mutinying while I'm gone? It's relevant. There are belongings I'll take with me if I should expect to discover the ship missing when I return."

He fell silent, then his ears twitched. Amusement swept over him in a visible wave—the lift of his whiskers and the curve of his mouth into an irrepressible smile. "No. I've considered it, but only to spite you for thinking I'd do it."

"Well then, I have what I need." I tightened the drawstrings of the sack. I turned and grasped his forearm. In return, Starkey's hand locked about my bicep in a fast hold.

"Does this mean I can come with you?" he asked.

"No." We traded grins and dissolved into laughter.

"Jayden..." He shook his head, still chuckling.

"David, you were correct to challenge me and you are right to be angry. I have questioned your loyalty, and without cause. The fault is mine, and mine alone. I'm a damaged, distrustful creature.

There will always be times when I need reminding—you're my brother."

Starkey shook his head, sighed, and regarded me with a look which could only be described as pitying. "You're my captain."

"Take care of my ship while I'm away. Keep her safe."

This time, he didn't argue.

CHAPTER 11

Devil's Rock—Blackberry Bluff

Mid-morning sailing conditions proved ideal. I navigated the dinghy, a small craft equipped with a mast and sail, into the shoals. The Scythe Strait was a treacherous canal that ran between Devil's Rock and Albatross Cay, a barren stretch of sand and grass where sea birds nested. After I lowered the sail, the powerful current swept the dinghy straight past the gaping, toothy maw of Devil's Rock.

Devil's Rock—an oxymoron if ever I've heard one —was neither devilish in origin nor composed of stone. The merfolk told the legend of a titan who'd engaged a mighty battle with Poseidon. The titan had sustained egregious injuries and attempted to flee onto land. He came within two miles of shore when Poseidon's triton pierced his back. The titan toppled and sank to the depths. His skeleton rested on the ocean's bottom, concealed beneath the waves. His head, however, planted chin first atop a rocky outcrop—and there it remains to this day. The elements had long ago stripped the skull bare of skin and sinew, sun had bleached the bones, wind and water had worn them smooth. Seabirds nested in the nasal cavities, and the jutting jawbone concealed the entrance to a sea serpent's lair. In a final, lingering irony, Poseidon had cursed the titan to an eternity spent gazing through his empty eye sockets toward the main island... and the escape that had eluded him.

The waters south of Devil's Rock concealed untold hazards, including coral reefs, shifting sandbars, and cagey outcroppings that could eviscerate a vessel. Treacherous conditions stretched for miles well past the narrow mouth of Mermaid Lagoon. It'd have been suicide to sail *Revenge* into the shoals, but the dinghy skipped across the breakers, evading lurking dangers. When the Scythe Strait current weakened, I raised the sail again.

Another couple hours of easy cruising, and I reached my destination well before sundown.

Blackberry Bluff: a fingertip peninsula located a few miles south of Devil's Rock and north of Mermaid Lagoon. Patches of tough vines covered in wicked thorns crowned the cape. Biting insects swarmed the swampy air and crawled along the twisted creepers. Dense brambles concealed stinking sinkholes that would swallow a person whole in a matter of seconds, leaving no trace but a fat, bubbling burp. In summertime, the bright green stems drooped beneath the weight of shiny black fruit. Needle-sharp prickles lacerated the flesh of an unwary picker. Swollen drupes burst at the slightest touch, sticky and staining. The ripe fruit attracted birds, bears, boars, and pixies in droves.

Sounds unpleasant?

Maybe so, but mark my words, the plumpest, tastiest berries in all of Neverland grew there. The reward proved worth all those considerable risks. Those blackberries melted on the tongue, unleashing starbursts of tart sweetness. Years later, my mouth still watered to think of them. Blackberry Bluff remained one of the few places from my childhood in Neverland of which I retained reasonably good memories.

Every now and then, when nostalgia aligned with convenience, I returned to Blackberry Bluff. Sometimes, I insisted on visiting even when the journey took us weeks out of our way and incurred a considerable expense, simply because I wanted to. The crew seldom complained. Infrequently, a new recruit grumbled, but was promptly met with stern rebukes from the veteran members. At the quest's end, the crew anticipated treasure worth its weight in gold—bubbling tarts and flaky pastries straight from the galley ovens to the table. For a few days, we feasted like kings... In other words, ate ourselves sick. The excess fruit was treated, stored in barrels, and stowed in the deepest, coolest section of the hold. A few months later, the blackberry wine could be sold to the faerie folk for a pretty profit.

I suppose I've rambled off on yet another unrelated tangent. I've a tendency to do that. Now, where were we? Ah yes... the scheme that'd brought me alone in a dinghy to Blackberry Bluff.

I aimed to catch a pixie.

CHAPTER 12

Pixie Traps—Tinker Buzz

I placed the bundled handkerchief upon a flat boulder, untied the corners, and smoothed out the linen square. It held three petite desserts, which had been specifically prepared by the ship's cook. Now, Frenchie had no formal confectionery training but I must applaud his efforts, for he truly outdid himself. The offering included a glazed cake the size of my thumbnail, a zesty lemon macaroon, and a chocolate-caramel truffle dusted in sugar. As I laid them out, the tempting aroma wafted to fill my nostrils and set my stomach to rumbling. Since I'd last eaten at dawn, and the exertion of the trip had left me famished, I regretted not having instructed Frenchie to pack extra.

Having artfully arranged the pastries upon the hanky, I extracted three silver thimbles. Delicate tasks requiring deftness and dexterity always challenged both my hook and my patience. I managed to spoon droplets of honey into one, however, and strawberry preserves into a second. All without making a huge mess, either. Heavy cream was the preferred beverage for baiting faerie traps, however the only source of dairy aboard *Revenge* was an old nanny goat named Mathilda. She produced milk so sour it turned saints to satyrs, and thus, was only suitable for making cheese. So, I filled the third thimble with cooled green tea and hoped for the best.

Trap baited, I faced away from the boulder, leaned my back against its smooth side, and propped my elbows on bent knees. I dug out my flute—a side-blown instrument made of ebony with silver keywork. It had a penetrating voice well suited to my assertive nature. I'd tried more subtle-sounding flutes, but none had felt right. I placed my lips near the opening and blew out the first experimental note.

With a bit of coaching, the flute produced a gentle lullaby. Swiftly, I lost myself in the tune. It should be noted that despite my passion, I loved music more than music loved me. But while I lacked Mr. Brown's ingenious talent, I was not wholly bereft of skill. Thanks to Virgil's dedicated tutelage, I had become quite adept at one-handed fingering on several different mediums, including the flute and guitar. If even the remotest possibility existed that an instrument could be played with a hand and hook, I was game to give it a go.

Merfolk crafted dark enchantments with their voice. It was not unlike Pan's ability, though I'd never discovered solid proof of a connection. The consequences to myself, however, were well established and cumulative—every time I sang, I surrendered another shred of my humanity and transformed a little more into a siren. I avoided doing so at all costs.

I played for well over an hour, wandering from one sweet song to another. Once I exhausted my limited repertoire, the cycle repeated. My fingers tired; my lips wearied. The whole time, I strained my hearing, hoping to pick up on any noise from behind me. Being half-deaf, listening proved a test of my patience. The temptation to glance over my shoulder persisted... like that itchy spot on one's back just out of reach. I dared not turn around, though. If my trap had worked, an interrupted sprite would flee, never to return.

The sun sank behind the horizon about the same time my fingers finally cramped up too badly to continue. With a gasp, I lowered the flute and panted, a bit winded from the exertion. I bent and shook out my hand, but delayed turning around just yet. A great deal depended on the trap's success, so I fretted over its potential failure. Only a pixie could tell me what I needed to know.

Two weeks had already been lost to the necessity of delivering the captured Lost Boys to Rackham's Cay. Of course, I could've kept them on board, but their proximity would've inspired Peter to attempt rescue, over and over, until he succeeded or someone died. The distance created an insurmountable barrier. By now, Pan, with his ephemeral memory, had already forgotten their names... maybe their very existence.

Now, it might seem I had more concern for the girl than the male children, but my bias derived from good cause. In Pan's company, girls weren't the same as boys. Their stint was finite, measured in weeks rather than years, or until Peter tired of the courtship. I wondered about that pretty girl, with her chestnut curls and her periwinkle frock. What was her name? Did she have a family? Was she still alive?

An owl hooted, startling me from drowsy contemplation. My chin slipped off my hand and my face dropped before I caught myself. Brooding, bah! A pastime suited to morose, moody elves! I straightened and stretched, working the stiffness from my limbs.

Moonlight shone over Blackberry Bluff, which meant I'd nodded off for an hour, at the least. I was fortunate I hadn't been attacked while I dozed. It'd be a miracle if a pixie hadn't stolen the bait and slipped the snare. Urgency jolted me into motion. I twisted around to face the stump where I'd laid my trap.

It'd worked.

A male sprite dozed on his tummy amidst the scattered crumbs. He measured less than six inches from the tips of his delicate antenna to the soles of his petite feet. A tuft of tawny hair topped his small head. Bumblebee stripes covered his plump torso, which tapered to a sharp, dangerous stinger. He had two pairs of diaphanous wings, longer on top. Glistening honey and jam smeared his mouth and hands. Sweetly oblivious, the sprite sawed out an unbroken stream of snores.

A small golden charm in the shape of a bumblebee lay on the handkerchief beside him. Now, every pixie has a soul charm, but they are kept well hidden and fiercely guarded. I pinched the ornament between my fingernails and lifted it for closer inspection. Intricate etchings decorated the bee, anatomically correct down to the gold thread hairs on the legs. When shaken, it emitted a vibrant buzz. I closed my fingers around it for safekeeping.

I dipped my chin and blew softly on the slumbering sprite. The current stirred his wings. He grunted and bunched his limbs tighter, holding fast to sleep. When I inhaled, the sweetness of clover flooded my nostrils. The scent instilled a sense of tranquility and timelessness. If I'd closed my eyes, it'd have taken little effort to envision a verdant meadow full of spring grasses and wildflowers.

"Wakey wakey."

"What?" He had a high-pitched voice that challenged my hearing. I turned my face, bringing my left ear closer.

"It's time for you to wake up."

"Go away." He waved his hand and rolled onto his side, facing away from me.

"Not bloody likely. We have business to discuss, you and I."

"I don't know you." He pried open heavy eyelids and gawked up at me. From his perspective, I imagined I appeared as a bear would to a mouse—big and blurry.

"I'll properly introduce myself once you arise. Now get up." I nudged him gently with the side of my hook. I worried about harming such a fragile creature unintentionally, but the matter needed quick resolution. Inevitably, urgency seemed to be the lock, stock, and barrel.

"I'm up! I'm up!" Covering a yawn with his hand, he stumbled to his feet. "Now, who are you and why are you so bothersome?"

"Captain Jayden Hook, at your service. In answer to your latter query, I suppose I was born bothersome, though opinions on the matter may vary."

"*The* Captain Hook?" the sprite yelped and launched into the air. His wings beat so fast they blurred and produced a thrum, like an angry wasp. Like most pixie folk, he wore little in the way of clothing—a brown girdle and cockleshell clogs. Tiny implements and numerous pouches hung from the utility belt. No doubt, those purses held more tools and crafting materials than they looked capable of containing. Fae magic was deceptive like that: able to warp perception, space, and sometimes even time.

"The one and only. And you are?" I rolled my hook, pantomiming a courtier's flourish. Barnacles, but I hoped he didn't intend to challenge the veracity of my identity. I'd had quite enough of that nonsense.

He hovered level with my face. His aura shed the lime-green shimmer which signaled fear. "Tinker Buzz. That's the Clan Tinker, of which I'm a member. I go by Buzz which is the sound I make but also who I am, a complex thing which often confuses outsiders—"

"So, Buzz it is," I said with a touch of impatience. I was familiar with sprite nomenclature and had no desire to listen while he explained it.

"Rude much? Asking me questions, then cutting me off before I even get a word in edgewise! What manner of rough-hewn ruffian are you?" Buzz waved his fists and aimed his stinger at my eye.

"Well, I am a pirate, but I've never been accused of garrulous grandstanding." Reflexively, I brought up my arms to defend my face from attack.

The careless gesture set off the golden bee secreted within my fist. It strummed in sync with the pixie's flight. Buzz jerked, his gaze drawn straight to my hand. His eyes rounded before he cast an alarmed glance down at the handkerchief. He scanned it frantically. Upon finding his soul charm gone, his aura underwent a crimson explosion.

"Thief! Wretch! Philanderer!" He swooped and I ducked out of the way. The angry pixie passed close enough to my cheek to allow me to feel the vibration of his rapid wings.

"I deny nothing."

Buzz dove at me, stinger first. I ducked aside, but barely. The sprite's current blew across my cheek. "You stole my soul charm! Give it back!"

"I did not, however, steal your charm." I tucked the ornament into a pocket and doffed my cavalier hat. This time I was ready. When Buzz swung around for another attack, I caught the angry pixie within my cap and sealed the sides together.

The hat vibrated with the force of his determined attempts to escape. Though muted through the leather, Buzz shouted curses and threats, demonstrating a truly impressive vocabulary. I stayed silent and held fast to the makeshift net, waiting while his tantrum played itself out. By their nature, sprites are volatile, passionate creatures. Their explosive outbursts tended to fizzle as swiftly as they ignited. It took Buzz about three minutes to wear himself out.

Instead of subsiding, though, he dissolved into sobbing.

My heart wrenched at the piteous sound. Carefully, I upended the cap over the handkerchief and the sad little pixie tumbled out. He landed on his bottom, hands clutched over his heart. His aura was deep blue and he'd lost one of his shoes. I shook the cavalier hat. The missing cockleshell cog tumbled onto the handkerchief beside him.

"Oh, stop your blubbering!" I snarled, smacking my hat back where it belonged. It crossed my mind a split second too late that the inside would be covered in honey and jam and crumbs... all now stuck in my hair.

I winced, but it was too late.

Buzz buried his face in his palms and wept harder. A nasty taste filled my mouth and I grimaced. Ah, wasn't I a fine and formidable villain? I proudly considered myself an exceptional buccaneer of questionable moral character, but even I have limits. Bullying a pixie was despicable even by my standards. Yet, here I was doing just that. I wanted to blame Pan for reducing me to this, same as I'd held him culpable for so much else, but the lie was too bold. I'd chosen to cross this line of my own free will.

"Hush, will you? Please?" I tried to moderate my tone, but suspect I achieved nothing more than a wretched parody of gentleness. "I mean you no harm. I only wish to talk."

"I don't want to talk to you." He lifted his chin in defiance. Snot and tears mixed with the honey and jam. It was... revolting.

"No reason you should. Your reluctance is why I made the offering." I extracted a second clean handkerchief from my sleeve and offered Buzz the corner of the square. At first he rejected the gift, but when I nudged him again, he latched on and clutched the hanky in his arms.

"You tricked me!" Buzz hiccupped the accusation.

"Balderdash. The trade was fair 'n' square. It's not my fault you've regrets now that the feast is consumed." I snorted. I had plenty of reasons for remorse, but not for this. "I obeyed the rules. You accepted my favor. Now you owe me a favor to buy your soul charm back."

"Scourge!" He hurled out a few more wildly creative curses to which I readily agreed. One, I thanked him for. Afterward, he crossed his arms over his rotund chest and settled to pouting. "What do you want from me?"

"You must answer a few questions first so I may determine the exact nature of the favor to be performed." I chose my words with precision, because the situation mandated it. Fae, even generally benevolent creatures like pixies, were cunning. If I wasn't careful, he'd find some way to escape through trickery.

"I'm not obligated to tell you anything for free."

"No, you're not. However, without the information I need, I'll be forced to wait until I can determine what to ask for. Of course, you'll have to accompany me. I've no objections to having a mascot about. In fact, I was considering acquiring a parrot. How would you feel about perching on my shoulder?" I tapped my hook against the epaulette of my brocade jacket.

Buzz wound up and spat to express his opinion. "How many questions?"

And so, the negotiations began.

CHAPTER 13

Bartering—A Deal Is Reached

How many questions did I have needing answers? That was a good question right there. I pursed my lips and pondered. Off the top of my head, I could list six specific inquiries that required explanations, but there were a great many unknowns. I preferred to hedge my bets.

"Twelve questions to which you must provide honest answers," I said.

"No way." He shook his head. "Three."

"I'll meet you in the middle—nine."

Buzz screwed up his round face in thought. He worked his fingers like an abacus. From the stubborn thrust of his jaw, he wanted to argue for the sake of arguing... and doubtless he hungered for the taste of victory. He wanted to outwit me and beat me at my own game. At the same time, he was clearly confounded. Poor fella. Not his fault most sprites can't perform arithmetic.

"Hah! You're trying to trick me again!" Buzz shouted at last. "No more of your skullduggery, scoundrel! I'll answer eleven questions and not a single one more! That's my final offer. Don't bother trying to talk me higher!"

"Ah, well, you caught me," I said with a sheepish smile. "Very well, eleven questions to which you must provide honest answers. You, sir, drive a hard bargain."

"That I do." Buzz preened proudly, and his aura turned peacock blue. I allowed him a minute to gloat, mostly because I still suffered the lingering sting of guilt over having made him cry.

We repeated the bargain and hammered down the wording. Then, I extended my fingertip and we shook on the deal. "First question. Where has Pan hidden the sailing ship, *Ariel*?"

Buzz faltered. "I can't tell you that! Peter Pan will smash me flat if he finds out I snitched."

I'll smash you flat. The shameful threat crossed my mind, but not my lips. I bit my tongue to silence it. Instead, I said, "Pan won't find out. Not from me. Not unless you tell him. Per our agreement, you must answer honestly."

He heaved a deep sigh. "Fine. Peter has his ship moored in the largest sea cavern of Crocodile Cove."

Crocodile Cove. The mere mention sent shivers coursing down my spine. The secluded bay was located at the northern edge of Neverland. The Tick-Tock Crocodile, the ravenous monster that had swallowed my hand and hungered still to consume the rest of me, lurked in the opaque waters. The mouth of DeNile flowed to and from the bay. The swift, deep river bisected the main island. Half of DeNile flowed north and the other half ran south, with a dead zone in the middle. Its contradictory current rendered it an ideal means of crossing the island swiftly, but only if one was willing to risk the man-eating reptiles lurking in the murky depths. I abhorred Crocodile Cove and avoided DeNile like the plague... which made it the ideal and obvious place to hide a schooner. As Pan damn well knew. It should've occurred to me immediately; it pricked my ego that it hadn't.

"What's your next question? Snap to it! I don't have all night!" Buzz sparked his aura so it produced a sharp crack.

"Tell me about the girl."

He paused overly long, and then donned a laughably contrived expression of innocence. "What girl?"

"The girl Pan stole!" I snapped. "Don't pretend you don't know who I'm talking about. Your aura turns orange when you lie."

"Biscuits!" He fell silent.

"Well?"

"You haven't asked a question."

Oh, right. I gnashed my teeth. Well, I had a generous cushion, so I asked, "What's her name?"

"Wendy Darling."

"Wendy..." I tested it on my tongue and liked how it rolled. It was an unusual name. I'd never heard it before, but when I paired it with my memory of the pretty girl in periwinkle, it fit.

Buzz fidgeted. "That's two questions. Is that all you needed?"

"Is Pan greatly enamored with Wendy?" I fished out the golden bee and held it so the sprite could see it. It worked like a—forgive the pun —charm.

Buzz's attention locked on it. He sparkled with effusive excitement. "Oh yes! Peter Pan adores her! He's quite taken with her. Wendy is delightful. When she sings, it's prettier than the mermaids. I've told her so, but she didn't believe me. Though she did say I was sweet and gave me a tulip—"

"Does Wendy like the mermaids?" Another throwaway question since it was about the same as asking if teenage girls loved horses. But I needed specifics to formulate a solid plan.

"Wendy *loves* mermaids! Peter accompanies her to Mermaid Lagoon almost every afternoon. Wendy always swims out to Marooners' Rock and tries to speak with them, but they won't have anything to do with her..." He trailed off, pouting.

"No, they wouldn't." Merfolk hold themselves above humans and disdain contact with outsiders. They also despised Peter Pan, but the eternal boy was too dangerous to ignore. Sirena, Queen of Sirens, loveliest of the nine mermaid queens, liked to keep close watch on her enemies. On her orders, the prettiest mermaids often lounged on Marooners' Rock, engaging Peter with flirtation and flattery.

Buzz frowned. I suspected I'd confused him.

"My apologies for the interruption. Please go on, tell me more about Wendy. Does she tell stories?" My chest constricted as though a great hand sought to crush the life from me. If Wendy happened to be a skilled storyteller, it would buy her extra time until Pan grew bored.

Long ago, I was an accomplished raconteur.

"Oh, yes! She tells the most wonderful stories! When she sits at the campfire, even the loudest lads quiet down and listen. Wendy is twelve, and has two younger brothers, John and Michael. John is eight and likes to wear a top hat. Michael is only five—"

"Five!" Nausea swirled in my gut. Neverland posed far too many dangers for a child of such a tender age. Peter usually chose older boys, those closer to independence and less needful of coddling. In his own words, Pan was intolerant of "crybabies and cowards."

"Yes, five." Buzz frowned and fell silent.

I scowled, pondering. Wendy this and Wendy that. From the way the sprite gushed on and on with effusive praise, the new girl was the belle of the ball. If Buzz had it right, and I had little reason to doubt him, Pan would be obsessed, which meant...

Tinker Bell would be *furious*.

"How does Tinker Bell feel about Wendy?" I

asked, seeking to confirm my suspicions. Better to be sure. Assumptions could prove deadly.

He turned lime green once again. In a tiny voice, he said, "The queen doesn't care much for Wendy."

"Tink must be sick with jealousy. I'll bet she's in a terrible temper over Peter lavishing all his affection on Wendy." I pressed my lips together to prevent the smirk struggling to rise.

Buzz hung his head and dropped his wings. "Peter and Tinker Bell fight constantly. Afterward, the queen goes on mead benders and hurls things. And she cusses up a storm."

This time, I didn't bother hiding my amusement. "Tink always did have quite the mouth on her. It sounds like she's taking it out on everyone *but* Pan."

He nodded woefully. "It's been awful. The entire clan is terrified."

"All that awful dissension over a girl," I said with false sympathy. "Would you like it to stop and for things to return to the way they used to be?"

"Yes, but..." Buzz stared up at me in sudden suspicion. His aura darkened to pumpernickel. "Are you offering to help? Why would you? I don't trust your motives! It's well known you're mean and cruel and—and—and..." He sputtered.

"Malicious might be the word you're looking for."

"Malicious!"

"That *is* my reputation; however, it doesn't change the situation in the least. You have a problem disrupting your life, and I desire to take that person away from Neverland. Our interests are aligned."

"I don't understand what you're saying, but I think you're up to more trickery. I don't even remember how many questions you've asked me." The brightness of unshed tears shone in his eyes and my conscience pinched.

"I've asked seven questions. There are four left."

Buzz blinked. "Only seven? We've been talking an awfully long time..."

"I've rather enjoyed our conversation, despite the unfortunate circumstances. I've often missed the company of sprites, these past few years."

He studied me long and hard before he said, "You're not what I expected, Captain Hook."

I tipped my hat to him. "Nor are you what I expected. To demonstrate my respect for our hard-won rapport, I'll speak plainly. My goal is to capture Wendy and spirit her away from Neverland. To do so, I need your assistance."

Buzz's pixie aura turned ashen. "No, I couldn't!"

"Why not? The girl has created terrible havoc.

Once Wendy's gone, things will go back to the way they used to be between Peter and Tinker Bell."

"But I don't want Wendy to go away! She's my friend. I love her!"

"If you truly love Wendy, as you claim, then all the more reason to help me save her. Do you want her to die just so you can have a few more weeks of her company?" Grim determination enveloped me. As an eternal cynic, I doubted any argument I made or any reason I gave could win the sprite's cooperation, but I had to try.

"What do you mean?" Buzz backed away, even though I'd not so much as lifted a finger against him. He was running from the truth, I suppose.

I leaned over so I could look him square in the eyes. "You know who I am, don't you?"

"Captain Hook." He trembled so swiftly his wings vibrated.

"I was an innocent girl when Peter Pan brought me to Neverland. I may be a monster now, but I am what he made me. You must have heard the stories—what he did to me. I know how sprites love to gossip."

"Peter Pan isn't a sprite." Buzz dropped his gaze.

"No, he's something older and darker, but that changes nothing. Tinker Bell has chosen Pan as her consort. Your people cringe from Pan's atrocities, but not a one of you does a thing to stop him, which makes you complicit."

"I have no power. I can't change anything."

"How would you know? You've never tried. Once, I had dozens of sprites I believed were my friends, but when Pan chained me, not a single one lifted a finger to help." In the moment, I imagined I glowed with an infernal light.

"Please stop." Buzz crossed his arms over his stomach. His halo thickened to pea soup. I despised myself for tormenting the poor pixie, but it had to be done.

"I won't. I can't. Inevitably, Peter will grow tired of Wendy, or she'll become a woman and her time will run out. Then, Pan will do to her what he did to me. If the girl is lucky, her death will be swift. If she's not..."

"No..." Buzz moaned, but rallied in defiance. "For all I know, you want to hurt Wendy. You're Captain Hook! You steal children and they're never heard from again."

"I swear, I've never harmed a child... never will. Every Lost Boy I've captured is safe, living on another island out of Peter's reach."

"How do I know you're telling the truth?"

"You don't. I could show you, but it's a two-day

trip across open water with prevailing winds. Would you be willing to go?" Sprites hated water. When their wings got wet, they couldn't fly, leaving them vulnerable.

Buzz shook his head.

"On my honor, my hand raised to death, I promise not to harm a hair on Wendy's precious head —or any other child, for that matter."

Still, he hesitated.

"You said Wendy is your friend. If that's true, if you're a real friend, then help me to save her. Please." I offered Buzz his soul charm. When he didn't reach out, I pressed it against his striped chest. This time, his arms automatically closed about the treasure.

"I don't understand." He clutched his charm and shed a tear.

"You fulfilled your side of our bargain. We're done. You're free to go." I flicked my hook skyward. No more coercion. If he chose to offer his assistance, it'd be of his own free will.

"What about Wendy? We have to save her." He dissolved into a sob. The golden bee vanished from his grip to wherever it was pixies hid them.

"You sprites... so emotional." With a sigh, I offered the cleaner of the two hankies. He latched hold, buried his face against the linen, and cried until he was exhausted. The outburst hit like a tempest and then blew over just like that, too.

"So, Hook," Buzz demanded, hands on his hips. "Do you have a scheme for catching Wendy, or do I have to do all the heavy lifting?"

"Oh, I have a notion."

CHAPTER 14

Mermaid Lagoon—Mr. Smee

Mermaid Lagoon lies south of Devil's Rock and east of the Dragon's Spine Mountains. Land surrounds the oval bay on all sides, except for a narrow passageway between two finger-thin peninsulas. Blackberry Bluff forms the northern point, and Currant Cape the southern. The mouth to the lagoon is too shallow for a ship to traverse without scraping bottom. A patchwork quilt of submersed rock formations, sandbars, and coral reefs stretches for miles.

SUMMERTIME, Pan's favorite season, occurred about ten times a year in Neverland, where even the climate was susceptible to Peter Pan's compelling charisma. The weather changed to suit his whims.

When the days grew hot and long, Peter and the Lost Boys often sought refuge in Mermaid Lagoon. There, they dawdled away countless hours, basking on the warm ivory sands. They swam in the emerald waters, played at being mermaids and pirates, and chatted on Marooners' Rock, a smooth isle set bullseye center in the round bay.

From a high sea cliff overlooking the lagoon, I watched through my spyglass. Children cavorted in the lagoon below. I counted them... or tried to. With frustrating regularity, I would reach a solid head count of eight before I had to restart. They darted through the shallows like a school of sardines, changed course at random, dove in one spot, and surfaced in another. In my paranoia, I imagined the youngsters thwarted my efforts through conscious design.

"How many boys are there, Captain?" Smee asked in that servile tone of his. It grated on my nerves so much, I cringed.

"Too many."

"Six?" Smee suggested with hopeless optimism.

"At least a dozen, and those are the ones we can see. There could be scores more spread out across the rest of the island."

Peter Pan's disposable coterie. No matter how many children I captured, it never seemed to do any good. Pan always found replacements.

"Dozens? That's not good, Captain."

"It is the opposite of good, Mr. Smee." Anger and frustration twined like serpents within me. My jaws ached because I'd been grinding them again. Dr. Chopp, the ship's surgeon who also doubled as our dentist since we lacked a proper barber, reproached me often about the bad habit.

"I could send Beaver to fetch the nets." Smee scrunched his nose, sending his spectacles sliding to a precarious perch on its bulbous end.

"It'd do no good. The second they see us coming, they'll vanish like little mice. We'd waste an entire day chasing them through the brush and be lucky to capture two." Spying was an exercise in futility. I collapsed the scope and stowed it. I had only kept watch this long in the hopes of spotting the girl, anyway.

"True, Captain."

I dragged a handkerchief across my brow to keep stinging sweat from my eyes and then toweled off the back of my neck. It came away sodden. An unusual and oppressive heat hung over Neverland. As a concession, I'd already shed most of the finery I favored, including my hat and jacket. My long-sleeve blouse and sash had followed, leaving me clad in a corset, a blouse, trousers, and boots.

It'd been five days since my initial meeting with Buzz. Since then, we'd arranged to rendezvous twice more to conspire. That seemingly innocuous sprite had proven shockingly cunning when he put his mind to it. Of course, niggling mistrust ate at me. It required force of will to silence the voice in the back of my mind that predicted he'd betray me. I repeatedly reminded myself of two things: sprites are terrible liars, and Buzz genuinely cared for Wendy. He wanted the girl to live... maybe more than me.

"Excuse me, Captain." Smee cleared his throat.

"Yes, Mr. Smee?" I cast my irritation at the interruption over him, which may not have been entirely fair. The bo'sun had also removed his hat, and the sun had baked his bald scalp dark red.

"Permission to speak freely?"

"Speak your piece." I lifted my hook in a go-ahead.

"I have reservations regarding your plan tomorrow evening."

"And what are those specifically?" My face hardened into a stony mask. Smee had just strayed into perilous waters.

Smee faltered, but then forged on. "It's too much effort for too little prize. We're expending a lot of resources to capture one girl. You yourself, you just said there are probably a few dozen boys in Neverland. It seems to me..."

"Go on! Speak plainly."

"It strikes me that you value the life of that girl more than the boys." Smee heaved for breath, but he lifted his chin in staunch defiance. As much as I disliked the bo'sun, I did respect his courage when it came to standing his ground.

Anger flashed through me, but I reined in my temper. "I don't value the life of one child more than another. However, I have chosen to make Wendy a priority specifically because she is a girl."

"I see," he said in a thin tone that indicated the opposite.

"I don't think you do. Most boys will survive years with Pan before they transform into beasts. Of course, there's always the risk that one of the island's many perils might kill a boy tomorrow, but that's an uncertainty. Wendy's future is measured in weeks, maybe."

"I understand Pan's wickedness," Smee interrupted. The bo'sun turned redder in the face than his sunburn could account for. No doubt he feared I meant to recount the salacious details for his benefit.

"Right, you do. We don't always see eye to eye, Mr. Smee, but so far we have managed to set our differences aside. Work together toward our common goal—"

"Saving children," we said in unison.

We traded a long look.

"I understand your position on the girl, Captain. Thank you for explaining. You have my full support." Smee snapped off a smart salute, which I returned. That exchange proved oddly gratifying.

I executed a neat turn and marched off, because I was eager to be underway. Though downhill, the return trek to Bright Bay where we'd left the dinghy would take an hour. Smee lagged behind, so I tarried. Our rare covenant bought him a full minute before my patience ran thin.

"Mr. Smee!"

"Coming, Captain!"

CHAPTER 15

Hard Truths—Sacrifices

After our return to *Revenge* in the dinghy, Mr. Smee retired for the evening. He stumbled off, mumbling beneath his breath like a walker already in the grip of slumber. The specter of fatigue sapped my strength and sleep beckoned like a tempting siren. Unease plagued my soul. In my current state, I would never find rest. The prospect of hours lost to tossing and turning dissuaded me from even trying.

The navigation room was a compact chamber located in the sterncastle, beneath the poop deck.

Floor to ceiling shelves held a myriad of tomes, mostly atlases, and *Revenge's* logs, and a walnut curio cabinet was overflowing with a wealth of maps and charts. The solid oak writing table, covered in nicks and scrapes, its finish worn thin, had as much character as any member of the crew. It stood on an aged wool rug that'd once been white, but now was the color of dust. The mat concealed a hatch that led to the great cabin in the level below.

The area had that wonderful aroma of old books: coffee and chocolate, sweet and musky, a scent that wafted into one's nose and lingered. Aside from the great cabin, it was my favorite place on the ship—where I went when I wanted to be alone.

In the grip of a dark and dreary mood, I locked myself away in the navigation room with my designs, devices, and private demons. Engrossed in those plots and plans, I lost all track of time.

A solid rap sounded on the closed door to the sterncastle.

My heart thudded in my chest, and I was jarred from my reverie and restored to awareness of the outside world. A sharp inhalation filled my airways with the scent of wet ink—sooty and astringent, but also an underlying hint of mild nuttiness.

I managed to lift my hand without smearing the writing. When I straightened, an aching spasm radiated through my lower back. My hand cramped, too. No telling how long I'd been standing there, bent over the journal. Presumably, it'd been some time considering both pages of the open journal were full.

The knock came again, stronger and urgent.

"Captain, are you still alive in there?" Starkey demanded from outside. He started to turn the handle without waiting for an answer.

"No, I'm quite dead. I'll thank you to knock before you come bursting in on me," I snarled. I thrust the quill into the canister and corked the fountain, but left the journal open because the ink needed to dry.

"I did knock." Darkness filled the portal, swallowing Starkey's prominent profile so not even a distinct silhouette could be distinguished. The emerald glow of his gaze peered out of the gloom.

"And then you burst without so much as a 'by your leave.'"

Starkey snickered. "May I please come in... by your leave, *El Capitan?*"

I gave an impatient wave. "Close the door behind you."

He stalked through the entry and shoved the door shut. In the lamplight, his orange-and-black fur shone. With the addition of the first mate's considerable bulk, the already tight area seemed much smaller. He studied me intently, and broke the silence with an observation of the obvious.

"You're burning the midnight oil."

"It's well past midnight," I said, waspish with weariness. I stretched my arms overhead in an attempt to ease the ache in my shoulders.

Starkey padded over to the writing table, crossing the compact chamber in a few long strides. His curious gaze roamed over the map of Neverland spread out on the surface. A brass-framed domed compass was positioned over the northernmost tip of the island. He leaned over to study it and I tensed. The crimp in my lower back worsened.

"Crocodile Cove, huh?" Starkey asked, glancing up. "Are you planning to visit?"

My face was as stiff as brittle parchment. I feared a smile might split my cheeks, but I forced one anyway. "Why yes, I thought it'd make a jolly good spot for a holiday."

He swished his tail. "You're kidding."

"That's me, jokester extraordinaire."

Starkey snorted. "I'm not buying it. You despise Crocodile Cove."

"With good reason," I ground out, mentally clenching *both* my fists—a routine dating from when the loss was still fresh and I could still feel my phantom hand. As the years had progressed, I'd mostly ceased the practice. In times of great stress, however, I caught myself reverting to old habits.

"I'd never suggest otherwise," Starkey returned with startling mildness.

The knots in my gut unraveled somewhat. The marvelous benefit of our friendship was never having to explain myself. It made what came next all that more difficult, but it had to be done.

Scowling, I broached the volatile matter. "Peter Pan has *Ariel* harbored there, secreted in the largest cavern."

Starkey's ears sprang sharply forward. He leaned closer. "Are you sure?"

"Absolutely."

"What's the source of your information?"

"A pixie. And before you say it—yes, I know what that's worth. He was under a contractual obligation to tell the truth, however. I'm confident the intel is correct."

Starkey narrowed his eyes, glinting brightly. "This is the same pixie who told you about the girl?"

"The same," I said, nodding. The tension returned with a vengeance, and I braced for a fight. Hours of preparation did nothing to lessen the sickness. "His name is Buzz."

"How long?"

The terse inquiry required no elaboration. I understood his meaning, but still I hesitated. Detestable honesty... such an inconvenient bother. For Starkey's sake, our mutual trust, and the strategy, however, I had committed to full disclosure.

"Five days."

"I see..." Starkey scowled and clenched his fists. He sank into a crouch as though to spring. When it came to emotions, the first mate had always read like an open book. When his ire sparked, igniting his temper, I hastened to cut the fuse before it burned down.

"You don't understand, Starkey."

"Oh, I think I do. I thought we'd settled this, but here I find out you've kept *Ariel's* location from me on purpose. Why would you keep important information like that from me—"

"Captain's prerogative. I was thinking—"

He got in my face. "Or you still doubt my loyalty. You lied when you said we were good."

"I've lied, but for none of the reasons you think, you thick-witted chump." I brought my hook up, smacking his chin with the smooth curve. Hardly more than a love tap, but it knocked him back.

His jaws snapped closed. He stumbled but recovered. A low, dangerous snarl rolled from his throat and his wicked claws sprang from their sheaths.

"I don't want you to leave," I spoke fast, unscripted words, spilling my figurative guts before evisceration became a literal reality for one or both of us.

Starkey missed a beat. His face was a blank canvas. I knew he'd heard, but feared he didn't believe. To demonstrate my sincerity, I dropped my hook and placed my hand on his wrist, leaving myself open to attack.

"When John left, it was devastating. He's been gone for years, and I still feel the loss. Losing you would be far, far worse."

Starkey's jaw dropped, and he stared as if he didn't know me. His claws retracted and he swayed; a strong wind would've blown him over. It was the only time I'd ever seen David completely flabbergasted.

"You're kidding," he managed finally.

"Ah, yes. Well, we established my penchant for chicanery."

"You'd miss me—more than John?" Starkey's whiskers lifted. He gathered smugness and momentum, and an alarm sounded in the back of my mind. This self-satisfaction must be stopped cold or he would become insufferable.

"Sorely missed. I am speaking as your captain, of course."

Starkey's ears twitched. "Of course."

I continued briskly. "Good officers are rare and valuable. Why, Mr. Rackham was scarcely competent and yet we went through four second mates before Mr. Mullins joined the crew. You're an exemplary first mate, Mr. Starkey. I dare say you're irreplaceable."

My grip slipped from his wrist and fell, but Starkey caught my fingers and squeezed. He grinned, baring his teeth, and shook with silent laughter. "Why, thank you, Captain."

Greatly discomforted, I withdrew and turned away. Lantern light glanced off the domed lens of the magnifying glass. Avaricious for a change of topic, I seized on the excuse to return to my obsession: Peter Pan.

Into the disquietude, I continued, "Pan must be deprived of that ship and the girl. The best strategy—with the greatest probability of success—is to take him unaware. I propose a two-pronged attack. We should deprive him of both prizes simultaneously. Peter can't be in two places at the same time. Even if he should thwart one of our raids, the other is bound to succeed."

"You're proposing we split up?" Starkey asked. He had his guard up. I could tell from the way he canted his head. I'd given him a lot to mull over. Whether he stayed or went remained to be seen... the decision was his to make now.

"You've been bellyaching about wanting an adventure..." I tapped the map, indicating Crocodile Cove. "This is your opportunity. I want you to choose three of the crew to accompany you. Former lost boys who are familiar with Neverland's terrain would be best. Predators capable of traversing the treacherous terrain. Not—"

"Beaver," we finished in unison, and then shared a good chuckle.

Starkey lashed his tail. "So your solution to

worrying I might leave is to toss me straight into the arms of temptation?"

"I loathe equivocation." *Temptation, mmm...* Now there was a name that brought a smile to my lips. It would do my boy some good to spend some time in that particular siren's embrace.

"Aren't you worried I won't come back?" he taunted.

I smirked. "Sooner or later, stray cats always turn up."

CHAPTER 16

Pearl Grotto—The Girl Who Loved Mermaids

On the night of the quartered moons, I took ashore a party consisting of myself and two others, Mr. Byron and Mr. Keats. The two men were the best of mates. We moored the dinghy in Bright Bay, which was south of Mermaid Lagoon, and proceeded on foot. Now, a system of underground chambers riddled the bluffs surrounding Mermaid Lagoon. Most of the time, the caverns were flooded, but when the tide ebbed, the system drained.

On the first stroke of the Devil's hour, we entered a narrow tunnel along the western bluffs of Bright

Bay. It faced west, but eventually led north. I knew those caverns like the curve of my hook, so I led the march. Byron and Keats followed, and we trekked single file for several miles through the winding underground labyrinth. Our bullseye lanterns provided much-needed illumination, but the hike was still a perilous one.

Saltwater got trapped in nooks and crannies in extensive tidal pools, which were home to crabs, snails, and a myriad of other creatures. I would frequently take a step only to feel something crunch and squish beneath my foot. The tunnels were cold and damp, and the gag-worthy rankness of rotted fish cloyed the atmosphere. Slick scum covered the rocks, and the corridors secreted pitfalls and projections. A single misplaced step could end a life, which was why the clumsy, nearsighted Mr. Smee had remained behind on the ship.

An hour later, we reached our destination. I halted outside the concealed entrance to Pearl Grotto. Throughout Neverland, there existed peculiar luminescent seaweed which grew in thick curtains and cast an eerie blue nimbus. One of those living drapes hung before me now.

"Why're we stopping, Captain?" Mr. Byron asked loudly.

"Obviously, we're stopping because we've arrived, you ninny. Drop your voice. We're supposed to be being stealthy," Mr. Keats answered at a near-shout.

"Shut up. Both of you," I snarled in the grip of irritation, having just spent the last hour listening to the two of them bicker like an old married couple. Also, I questioned the wisdom of having brought company at all. If the plan I'd devised with Buzz unfolded smoothly, I wouldn't need them.

In my experience, however, things never went according to plan. Right off the top of my head, I envisioned a dozen scenarios where calamity could strike. What if, for instance, Wendy brought her brothers along instead of coming alone? One of the Lost Boys might follow her... or Pan. Or Buzz could've betrayed us, and *we* were about to walk into a trap.

I faced Byron and Keats, and communicated via sign language. "Wait here. Keep your nets handy. Dim the lanterns and no more talking. After I enter the grotto, you're to open a slim part in the sea tangle through which to listen. Don't allow it to close or you won't be able to hear anything happening within the grotto. You're not to reveal yourself unless I call. Understood?"

"Aye, aye, Captain," they answered in unison. When they closed the hoods on the lanterns, the blue glow filled the passageway.

Prepared for a fight, I dropped my hand to the hilt of my cutlass. I parted the kelp curtain with my hook and ducked through. Pearl Grotto, an orb-shaped cave, was a natural anechoic chamber. It amplified incoming sounds, but muffled outgoing noise. In other words, it was near impossible to sneak up on anyone within the cave, and equally difficult to tell whether or not the grotto was already occupied.

The moment I passed the algae, I ducked right and searched for hidden threats. Nothing greeted my gaze, save for the smooth surface of the grotto's mineral spring. Wisps of steam floated above the water. The sharp temperature spike smacked me with my first indrawn breath. Humidity condensed into droplets on my bare skin. On the opposite side of the cavern, more sea tangle concealed another passageway, which led to Mermaid Lagoon.

I expected Wendy and Buzz to come from that direction.

We'd arrived two hours prior to dawn—the appointed time—so I settled in to wait. I chose a spot on the basalt shelf beside the pool. In anticipation of the heat and humidity, I'd left my jacket and hat on the ship. Even so, the air was sweltering, and within minutes my hair and clothing were plastered against my skin. The desire to strip and slide into the inviting pool tempted me, but I resisted. The risks simply outweighed the rewards. Instead, I stirred the water with my hook and watched the ripples spread.

Time passed.

Amplified voices from the Mermaid Lagoon tunnel rousted me from my reverie. With a huff, I hefted my chin and turned my head. Before their words became coherent, I managed to determine their identities. Buzz emitted a high, vigorous drone, and there was a distinctly female voice.

Pleasant surprise washed through me to discover the sprite had kept his side of the bargain. I sat straighter and composed myself, taking care to ensure my hook remained concealed behind my body. Thoughts still sleep-muddled, I reached for the hat that wasn't there, and my fingers passed through emptiness.

Shuffling footsteps drew closer.

"Through here. It's not much farther," Buzz said.

"Are you sure it's safe?" Wendy spoke in a soft, sweet soprano. Even though I'd prepared myself, finally hearing her voice disturbed me more than it should. Before, on the schooner, while in the grip of

Peter's spell, she'd seemed more a doll than a person. This made her real, somehow.

"Of course it's safe. I wouldn't do anything to lead you into danger! You do want to meet a mermaid? This is your chance! She's waiting right on the other side of this seaweed. You trust me, don't you?" Buzz gave a twittering laugh.

I winced. A shout got caught in my throat. It took an act of willpower to keep quiet. Although, belatedly, I remembered that I could've hollered at the top of my lungs and they still wouldn't have heard me.

The girl delayed answering. Waiting was like watching the fuse on a bomb burn down. When she replied, nervousness edged her tone. "I do want to meet a mermaid, and of course I trust you... But you're behaving rather oddly. Are you afraid, my dear friend?"

Smart child. Suspicion and stubbornness were traits I admired greatly. After the incident on *Ariel* when she'd been quiet and malleable, I'd fallen into the trap of thinking of her as a distressed damsel to be saved. Here she demonstrated insight and cunning all wrapped up in one seemingly innocent question. It forced me to revise my estimate of Wendy upward.

"Sure, I'm scared. Mermaids aren't just pretty girls with fish tails. They're quite terrifying," Buzz returned smoothly. Mentally, I applauded his deft recovery. I hadn't thought the little sprite had it in him.

"How so?" Wendy asked, sounding thoroughly intrigued.

"You should ask her yourself. Come meet her." Buzz grunted and the seaweed curtain moved a little, but not enough to part the strands. His pixie aura shone through the kelp, brighter than the bioluminescence.

I shifted, drawing my knees against my chest, and considered rising. Being seated put me at a disadvantage in regard to catching the girl if she decided to flee. The goal was to capture Wendy, preferably without terrifying her. The position was less threatening, though, so I stayed put.

"Let me help you with that," Wendy said. The sea tangle parted, and the girl poked her head through with the restraint of a doe emerging from a woodland refuge. She had her face turned away from me and hadn't noticed me yet.

Resonant droning marked Buzz's flight. The sprite aimed for a narrow part in the seaweed. Perhaps he misjudged, or maybe he flubbed on purpose, but he collided with Wendy's head and got tangled in her hair.

"Oomph!" Buzz cried, throwing a shower of multi-colored sparkle that lit up the entire cavern. They created quite the kerfuffle.

"Ow! You stabbed me!" Wendy exclaimed, and stumbled forward into the chamber. The seaweed curtain dropped closed behind her.

"I'm sorry. I didn't mean to. I'm stuck."

"No, I'm the one who's stuck!" Wendy bent over and flipped her shoulder-length hair, setting her wealth of curls to bouncing. The maneuver sent Buzz cartwheeling like a runaway firework. He crash-landed on the smooth cavern floor.

Buzz picked himself up and brushed off his wounded dignity. "Ouch. I think I stung myself."

"That would be quite the accomplishment. Given your shenanigans, the pair of you ought to team up and join the circus," I said with a grudging smile, amused despite the severity of the circumstances.

Wendy gasped and whirled. Her hand flew to her throat. She asked, "Are you a mermaid?"

"I'm part mermaid," I said, beckoning her, and she crept nearer. I wondered if she was even aware of her approach. Her wariness reminded me of a feral cat—curiosity at war with caution. Even disheveled, the chit was a pretty child.

"But you have legs!" Wendy exclaimed, and now her hand shot to her mouth. "Oh! I'm so sorry! I didn't mean to offer offense—"

"None taken. It's a fair question. You see, I have legs because I'm only part merfolk. I was born human... like you." I cocked my head, studying her.

Wendy's diction placed her as hailing from somewhere in London. An odd pang of nostalgia ached in my heart, even though it'd been decades since I'd last been home. The slight oddity in the way she enunciated her Ls left me with a shred of doubt. I wanted to ask, but admitting to a familiarity with England would've led to more awkward questions—not to mention disrupting my mermaid mystique.

"Really? That's quite fascinating! Buzz, isn't that most intriguing?" Wendy's face lit up with fascination. She was quite the open book, her thoughts written on her face. It was safe to speculate that the girl wanted more than to simply meet a mermaid. She longed to *be* a mermaid.

What a foolish child.

Buzz huffed. "It's interesting, I suppose. Not quite fascination, and nowhere close to intriguing. Interesting, sure, I'll grant you that."

"Perhaps you did sting yourself, Buzz. Your head is looking rather swollen."

"It is?" Buzz squeaked and scampered to the edge of the pool. He leaned over, trying to find his reflection in the water.

"What's your name, girl?" I asked, since I wasn't supposed to know.

"Oh! I'm so sorry!" Her hand flew to cover her mouth. By now, her excessive demurring and apologies had begun to erode her original charm. I wrinkled my nose, thinking I'd have preferred Wendy to be sassier and feistier. In the meantime, Wendy bobbed and curtsied, lifting her periwinkle nightgown, which had begun to look quite grungy from weeks of constant use. "I am Wendy Darling."

"Jayden Cook." While it was my birth name, the words snarled on my tongue. It felt and sounded like a lie. Leaving off "Captain" introduced a whole new level of wrongness.

"It's a pleasure to meet you." She bobbled again.

"Sit. I'll tell the tale of how I went from being a girl much like you to the bonded blood sister of Lorelei, Queen of Storms, fiercest of the nine mermaid queens." I patted the spot beside my knee. The girl's constant standing gave me plenty of worry.

I was concerned one of her erratic shifts in position would lead her to notice my hook.

Fortunately, Wendy's eagerness to learn more about the merfolk superseded her sense of prudence. She plunked down with her calves tucked beneath her, and folded her hands on her thighs. "Oh, that would be delightful! Please, do tell me more."

"I'm not swollen at all, you lying two-pence pirate!" Buzz sprang into flight. Somehow, the thrum of his wings conveyed irritation. He stuck out his tongue. I winced and hoped the girl hadn't noticed the outburst.

No such luck.

Wendy's eyes rounded to platter-sized proportions. She turned toward Buzz. "W-w-what do you mean... p-p-pirate?"

"Oops." Buzz turned fuchsia with embarrassment.

"Oops is right." Wasn't that just a slap to the face? I suppose I shouldn't have been surprised. Keep company with clowns, join the circus.

"Buzz, you sold me out?" Wendy asked with a heartbreaking tremor. Tears brightened her gaze and her lower lip trembled.

"I'm sorry!" Buzz turned blue and sobbed. He gushed out an incoherent stream of noise, which I suspected was an explanation or perhaps an endless apology.

"Well, as they say, the jig is up. You probably won't believe me, but I'm sorry we won't be able to continue our conversation. I'd have enjoyed telling you about my life with the merfolk. It's a good story." I lashed out and caught hold of Wendy's wrist before she came to her senses and tried to escape.

"Let go of me now!" Wendy cried out and jerked away, but the child's strength was no match for mine. She twisted like a fish on the line. I didn't want to hurt her, but I dared not loosen my grip. It'd only been a couple minutes since Buzz had showered the girl in pixie dust. Any bruising she suffered was preferable to her escaping back to Pan and certain death.

"I can't do that, love. Can't have you flitting off now, can we?" I surged upright, dragging the girl with me. Finally, Wendy got a clear view of my hook. She turned deathly pale and in a small voice asked, "Captain Hook?"

"The one and only." I tensed, expecting her to make some absurd accusation or repeat some other falsehood she'd been told by Pan. It came as a relief when she spouted a predictable, if pedantic, protest.

Wendy jutted out her pert chin. "You won't get

away with this! Peter Pan will come to my rescue. He'll save me!"

"For your sake, pray he fails."

"Wendy, please let me explain," Buzz begged. He floated overhead with his tiny hands clasped together.

"No! I don't want to hear anything you have to say! As far as I'm concerned, you're not my friend any longer!" Wendy turned her face away.

Buzz wailed and shed more tears. His sobbing drowned out the familiar thrum of his wings. A thorn of guilt embedded in my side, even though I had done absolutely nothing to feel bad for. He'd chosen to help me of his own free will. The bite of onus ignited my temper. Anger demanded an outlet. Given the choice between taking it out on a sprite, a child, or grown men, I chose the lesser of three evils.

I faced the Bright Bay tunnel and roared, "Mr. Byron, Mr. Keats! Bring your lazy backsides front and center!"

A distinct delay followed. I began to question the competence of my men and suspected they'd allowed the kelp curtain to close despite my instructions. I took a stride toward the hidden entrance, and it burst open. Byron and Keats rushed out, tripping over each other in their haste.

Bumbling nincompoops.

Their blundering soured my stomach, especially when I considered that I'd chosen these two to accompany me because they had above-average competence.

Keats said, "Sorry, Captain. We—"

"I'm not interested in your excuses, Mr. Keats. Take hold of young Miss Darling's wrist—" I offered Wendy's arm to him.

"Yes, sir!" Keats reached for the girl with ham-handed strength.

"Gently!" I hoisted my hook. In the eerie kelp light, the blue steel gleamed something wicked.

"Yes, sir." Keats faltered, but then proceeded with more care. Custody of the girl transferred to the men. Wendy offered up strenuous remonstrations, but she was bound to wear herself out soon.

"Escort Miss Darling back to the dinghy. I'll catch up with you."

CHAPTER 17

Unlikely Compassion—Chief of Faerie Engineering

I stood in the entrance to Pearl Grotto, holding open the kelp curtains, and watched their departure. Common sense said I should abandon any thought of lingering and leave immediately. An inconvenient bout of scruples, however, anchored me there. Gods only know what possessed me—a plague of principles from which I fervently hoped to recover.

"Buzz, I'd like a word with you before I go." I glanced over my shoulder. My cheek smacked something bristly and a black-and-brown blur filled my vision. A cry tore from my throat, and I jerked my face aside, reflexively ducking away from what I mistook for an insect attack.

A heated surge propelled me to fighting readiness. When threatened, my foremost instinct always screamed fight before flight. I raised my hook, but hesitated because I preferred not to skewer myself.

"Don't attack! It's me! Buzz!" The shrieking sprite dove for cover against my throat, probably figuring I wouldn't risk ripping out my own jugular. It was a solid strategy and it worked well... at first.

"Nutmegs! Stop that! It tickles!"

"You tried to kill me!" Buzz ducked beneath my hair and burrowed toward my nape. The unfamiliar sensation of what felt like a huge bug set my skin to crawling, and the overwhelming urge to swat at him —*anything to make it stop*—grabbed hold of me. I had to smother the impulse.

"Don't be a dunce. If I'd tried to kill you, you'd be dead. Now get out of my hair," I snapped, twitchy and short-tempered.

"I can't! I'm stuck! Help!" He struggled beneath the mass of my braids, which were woven with hundreds of pearl beads.

"I swear, my life is a Greek comedy." My mouth twisted into what might've been a grimace or an ironic grin. Right then, in the grip of conflicted emotions, I wasn't sure exactly *what* I was feeling.

No, that was a lie. I had disgust aplenty.

"I don't understand! What's Greek?" Buzz's wingbeat had acquired a hornet-like thrum, reminding me of his sharp stinger.

"Hold still while I lift my hair." I gathered my braids, and held them up until the sprite escaped.

He climbed onto my left shoulder and made a great production of brushing himself off. His pixie aura turned beet red, and he demanded, "Why did you do that?"

"Me? So this is my fault, is it? You snuck up on me."

"I never sneak. I buzz everywhere I go." He beat his wings to make his point.

"I'm deaf in my right ear. You could've pounded a drum and I wouldn't have heard you." Not entirely true, but close. I do have *some* sensitivity remaining on that side. Regardless, it didn't excuse the fact I'd let him catch me unaware. My inattentiveness angered me. Such a lapse at the wrong moment could get me killed.

In typical sprite fashion, Buzz flashed from outrage to contrition in a wink. "Oh! I'm sorry. I didn't know!"

"It's not your fault. You didn't know," I said, grudgingly, "but from now on, approach on my left side."

"Got it." He drooped and turned misery-blue. Buzz was, I suspect, confronting an unenviable insight. He couldn't go home again, not after what he'd done.

A heavy, woeful silence descended.

I wanted to go, but I stayed. No matter how much I wished it, some part of me refused to abandon Buzz. The sprite was so goofy and good-hearted, it offended my swashbuckler sensibilities. But... he had courage in spades, and he'd kept his word, both things I greatly admired. If his people ever learned of his role in Wendy's abduction... it might get him into trouble. I applied a qualifier only because of Tinker Bell's chaotic temperament. The faerie queen could decide to lavish him with praise or send him into exile. It depended on a great many factors, including how happy Tink was to be rid of Wendy and her temperament at the moment of the reveal. There was also a guaranteed consequence... Should Peter Pan ever discover Buzz's betrayal, the repercussions would be cruel and lethal.

Buzz understood all these things, and had helped anyway. He'd chosen self-sacrifice and he'd earned my respect. Out there in the world of pirates, treachery abounded—strength was the law of the sea—and any display of humanity could be interpreted as weakness. Within Pearl Grotto, the only place in all the Neverlands where privacy was guaranteed, I had an opportunity to be something I am not.

Kind.

I tried to speak, but a lump had stuck in my throat, so I cleared it. At the rough sound, Buzz perked up his antenna. Golden sparkles swirled through his navy nimbus.

Ruthlessness becomes me, so I hardened myself. Stony-eyed glare. Flinty voice. Sneering mouth. Anything else would've appeared contrived. "Before I depart, I would like to make you a proposition."

"Yes? What sort of proposition?" Buzz eyed me with mixed hope and mistrust. Good, he'd better question the motives of a benevolent Captain Hook. I would've, too.

"First, I wish to state that thanks to my youthful sojourn with Pan's company, I am familiar with Tinker Clan's mechanical aptitude. I've long admired pixie ingenuity and resourcefulness."

"Uh-huh." He looked askance at me. Can't say I blamed him. It left me thinking that I ought to get to the point.

"I would like to offer you employment as my ship's engineer."

"Is this a mean joke? Like when you compared me to a parrot?"

"I apologize profusely for that. It was uncouth." I bowed, even though the sprite still perched on my shoulder.

"No more parrot jokes?"

"I swear I have no desire for a parrot. Feathers make me sneeze."

He huffed mightily. "Your hat has a feather plume!"

A fierce grin split the sides of my mouth, and I tipped my head in salute, because he'd caught me in the lie fair 'n' square. "Well done!"

Buzz smirked. "Thank you."

"Regardless, I dislike birds—messy things."

The pixie nodded and seemed to accept the excuse. "Don't you already have an engineer?"

"I do, but the woman currently filling the position is barely adequate. Truth be told, she's a bumbling dolt..." Oh, I anticipated epic trouble if what I'd just said ever got back to Cairstine Wright. The Scottish woman had a temperament every bit as fiery as her hair. I made a mental note to have a word with her in private at the first opportunity—a discreet explanation and, more importantly, a lavish bribe should make things right.

"If she's so incompetent, then how is she your chief engineer?" He glowed brighter, suspicion and sorrow receding.

"I'm beset by ineptitude on all sides. It's near impossible to find professionals who wish to be pirates. Mercantile and military vessels offer better rewards for less risk." I spun out the glib lies, turning flax to gold.

Buzz nodded eagerly, lapping it up. "This is a real position? With a rank and a title and a salary?"

"Your position would be that of a third mate. Pirates receive an equal share of the take, not a salary. Officers receive four shares."

He puckered his face, probably from the exertion of performing mental calculations. Ultimately, he shrugged and moved on. "And my title?"

"Chief of Faerie Engineering. Head of the entire department." I crossed mental fingers that I wouldn't have to hire another faerie just so he'd have someone to boss around.

"Chief of Faerie Engineering..." He repeated it himself twice more, and wound up nodding in approval. "I like the sound of that. What would be my duties?"

"Your duties?"

"My duties."

"Well..." My eyes threatened to cross from a lack of ready answers. Oh bother, why couldn't he just accept the offer and be done with it?

"This is a trick! You don't have any duties for me to perform!"

"Untrue! I make a habit of pondering before speaking, especially whilst engaged in a parlay. I'm the captain, and as a member of my crew, you will respect that!"

"Yes, ma'am!" He snapped off a sloppy salute.

"Sir!"

"What?" Buzz screwed up his face. Effervescent bubbles percolated in his aura, and the pressure built till he looked ready to burst.

"When you address me, the proper forms are Captain,' 'sir,' or any combination of those two. Do you understand?"

"Yes, sir!" He slapped off another travesty of a salute.

A burst of epiphany showed me the advantage of having this conversation now. It presented an opportunity to cut off future conflict between Buzz and Wright and the rest of the contributing and *real* members of my crew. As soon as the cruel thought crossed my mind, I winced. Buzz was right to doubt me. My fundamental nature was that of a wolf, vicious and bloodthirsty. Compassion didn't suit me at all, and even the unsettling insight wasn't enough to stop me.

"As Chief of Faerie Engineering, you'll have your own workshop. The dreary duties of ship maintenance will remain with the current, albeit inadequate, chief."

Buzz worked his mouth. "I suppose that's good."

"Good? It's excellent. As Chief of Faerie Engineering, it will be your responsibility to create inventions and devise innovations which will improve our effectiveness at pirating!"

"Oh! Oh! That sounds so exciting!" Buzz hummed with such enthusiasm that he shot straight off my shoulder.

"If you find the terms acceptable, we must shake. Do we have a deal?" I held out my hand and left the decision to him.

With a joyous shout, Buzz bumped off my fingertip. "Deal!"

CHAPTER 18

Captain Interrupted—Assault from Below

Immediately after our return to *Revenge*, I gave the order to weigh anchor. From Devil's Rock, we sailed northwest along the island's coastline. The plan called for us to join up with Mr. Starkey at coordinates a few miles north of Crocodile Cove. We had set the time of the appointment at midday, though the skies and sea seemed to have entered into a conspiracy to keep us from our destination. A counter-current and a powerful headwind obstructed our progress. The sun passed its zenith before we reached the halfway mark and we missed our rendezvous.

The tedious ordeal exhausted my patience. I stood vigil on the poop deck while Mr. Mullins handled the helm. Wendy remained all too eager to be rescued. The chit spared no opportunity to assure us that Peter would save her. Listening to her grew tiresome, so I had her escorted to the great cabin. There, Mr. Smee and Mr. Brown were to keep her entertained and under constant supervision. So long as Neverland lay off our port side, I anticipated Pan would mount a raid against us. To that end, the ship maintained a state of battle readiness—gun ports open, artillery prepped. The armory was unlocked; firearms distributed to the crew.

"Does sailing always take this long?" Buzz perched on my left shoulder. For a creature that despised water, the sprite had proven remarkably adaptable regarding his new home aboard a ship. He investigated his new surroundings with relentless curiosity and great enthusiasm.

"The duration of a journey depends as much upon the currents and the wind as the distance covered." I proceeded to explain the basics of how tacking into the wind allowed us to advance.

In the intervening hours, Buzz fielded a barrage

of questions, and I did my best to answer. Under normal circumstances, the interrogation would've irritated me to no end. *Not* training new recruits was one of the many advantages of being captain. For Buzz, however, I made an exception—initially because the distraction helped pass the time. The sprite was clever and savvy—*and he learned*—as evidenced by his successive inquiries. He challenged my assumptions and forced me to think. Quite unexpectedly, I caught myself enjoying our exchange.

Hours passed.

Finally, the mouth of Crocodile Cove came within sight. I scoured the vista through my spyglass. The skies yawned clear and blue beneath the late afternoon sun, and fat swells rolled across the ocean. Seagulls flew in force, chasing a school of sardines that turned the sea into a silvery, rippling carpet.

"Do you see them?" Buzz asked.

"No." Apprehension ran rampant through me. *Where are you, Starkey?* Had my first mate encountered difficulties? I'd sent Starkey and three of my people on a mission to a place so dangerous it scared *me*. If they'd been hurt or killed, I'd never forgive myself.

"If you want, I could fly high and see what I can

see..." Buzz made the offer in a high-pitched and hesitant voice. Obviously, the prospect of crossing open water frightened him.

I stirred, seriously tempted to accept his proposal. Sudden insight dawned, and I perceived a plethora of ways Buzz could prove useful. At last, I understood how wrong I'd been to call the sprite deadweight even in the privacy of my own thoughts.

"Captain?" Buzz tugged at the top of my ear.

"No, the wind is blowing at twenty-five knots. If you didn't get knocked from the sky, those gulls would gobble you up." I repositioned the spyglass to scan the horizon again.

"Captain! Miss Darling has escaped!" Mr. Brown staggered on deck. He ground to a halt and bent over at the waist, grasping his sides while he panted for breath.

"How could that tiny chit have gotten away from two grown men?" I roared the question.

Mr. Brown sputtered, "Well—"

"Don't answer. Incompetence begets excuses."

"I'm sorry." Mr. Brown hung his head, and his shame doused the flames of my temper. Even if he'd captured the girl, it was doubtful the frail old man possessed the strength necessary to hold her. Besides which, Virgil's duties were those of a minstrel, not a nanny. Any blame to be placed belonged elsewhere.

"It's not your fault. Where is Mr. Smee?"

"He's alive, but unconscious. The young lady took his pistol and cold cocked him across the back of the head. She stole the keyring and locked me in, but I have my own and so I was able to let myself out..." He patted his vest pocket.

Angry, impatient demands pushed into my mind, and I bit my tongue to stop from interrupting. I wondered why Smee had armed himself in the first place. I didn't wish the bo'sun dead, but any man foolish enough to lose his weapon to an adolescent girl *and* have it used against him...

He deserved a sound thrashing.

Mr. Brown continued his disjoined story. "Mr. Smee needs tending. I wanted to go straight to Dr. Chopp, but I also knew you had to be alerted. I was torn—"

"You did the right thing, Mr. Brown. None of this is your fault. Go fetch Dr. Chopp to the great cabin." I gripped his arm in reassurance.

"What about Miss Darling?" Mr. Brown lingered, unable to let it go.

"Her escape is an annoyance, but it hardly counts

as a disaster. While we're at sea, she has nowhere to go. She can hide, though we will find her eventually."

"Yes, that's a good point. I should have thought of that." Mr. Brown drew a deep breath; his manner was that of an intelligent person made to feel stupid. My sympathy for him increased in leaps and bounds.

Walking unsteadily, he headed off. Problem dealt with, I moved on to the next and got a ship-wide search started for the missing girl.

"So, what's next?" Buzz asked.

Tea topped my list...

Before I formulated a reply, *Revenge* endured a battering assault from below. *Revenge* shuddered, all five hundred tons of her. The deck lurched in a sharp jolt completely contrary to the way a vessel *should* move on the water. The wrongness of it grated across my nerves. I'd spent years living on a ship. I'd kept my footing on rougher seas, ridden out storms that threatened to tear the vessel apart, and nothing in my repertoire had disturbed me half as much as this.

The crew knew it, too. Absolute stillness descended over the ship. No one so much as murmured, but I *felt* their collective shout in my bones.

Aggression coursed through me, that heating of the blood and desire of limbs to take action. The compulsion proved so powerful, tremors shook me. I stilled myself through an act of discipline and assumed a ready stance. My gaze fixed on the deck, and I waited pensively to see if the phenomenon would repeat.

"What was that?" Buzz fluttered his wings with anxious energy.

"I don't know."

"Could it have been a whale?"

"Not a snowball's chance on a summer beach, but you're headed in the right direction. That shock originated from below."

"Did she scrape bottom, sir?" Mr. Mullins asked.

"No, she didn't. The ocean floor here is more than a league deep." I'd experienced scraping bottom, too, and this wasn't that. I had a niggling suspicion about what it might be, but I preferred not to speculate.

"Your orders, Captain Hook?" Mullins asked.

"Stay the course and pass the word. Tell the chief engineer to meet me on the main." Foreboding hung over me like a guillotine, an inescapably bad feeling.

"Aye, sir!" Mullins relayed the command.

"I thought *I* was supposed to be your chief engineer?" Buzz's pixie aura turned querulous ochre.

"Now's not the time for petty rivalries. The

survival of the ship may depend on your ability to work with Wright."

"Oh!" Buzz shivered and didn't say anything more. Just as well, because my mood had turned gloomy. I'd brought Buzz on board with the anticipation there would be hiccups between him and Wright. I was prepared to work through it with them, but I'd also expected to have more time. As it stood, the pair hadn't even met yet.

Things were about to change fast.

I descended to the main deck, a trip that felt like an eternity. Buzz rode on my shoulder, uncharacteristically quiet, which made the thud of my steps seem all that much louder. The crew followed my every move. The burden of their gazes—and seventy souls—pressed down on me. Their lives and the ship depended on my judgment.

The disruption came again, same as before, but harder. This time the collision struck the underside and at the stern. *Revenge* shivered her timbers beneath the strain of the assault. She groaned in agony and I moaned in sympathy. A ship was the same as a living creature, except she had wood and steel in lieu of blood and bones.

Once the deck evened out, I hurried across to the port side. Cairstine Wright joined me against the railing. She smacked her hands onto the ornate taffrail and leaned out, mirroring my stance. Side by side, we stared into the ocean. The water, which had been teaming with millions of fish moments before, was smooth as silk... save for one thing.

A column of bubbles gurgled to the surface. Buzz hopped from my shoulder to my wrist and perched on the curve of my hook. His shimmer lent a magical glow to the steel.

"This is bad, Captain?" Wright spared Buzz a brief glance. Her stoic facade slipped, revealing her curiosity and mistrust. Neither reaction was unexpected or unreasonable. Cairstine had grown up in the all-human community on Rackham's Cay, and machines interested her more than people. She had little experience with her own people... and even less with faerie folk.

"Worse than bad. Chief Wright, this is Chief Buzz, our new head of Faerie Engineering." I gestured between them by way of introductions.

"Faerie Engineering?" Wright snickered. She smiled with her eyes, and even her frizzy hair crackled with hilarity.

"That's correct. Faerie Engineering." I leveled a mean stare, daring her to make a mockery of *my* pixie.

She stiffened and snapped her mouth shut.

"See that?" I aimed my hook at the churning spot on the otherwise smooth sea. By now, I suspected the identity of the creature troubling us, but I had no definitive proof beyond that turbulence. Well, *that* and the niggling suspicion worming its way through my gut. My frustration with our hidden enemy mounted.

"Something must be done to force the beast to the surface," I said, unintentionally voicing my thoughts aloud. "But what? How does one destroy an underwater enemy?"

It'd been a rhetorical question, but Wright and Buzz both agreed with profuse enthusiasm that they did indeed perceive it, too. I bit back a snarl of annoyance and muted a reprimand since there wasn't time.

The aspect of an enormous snake rose to right below the surface and swam broadside to the ship. For ten seconds, a serpentine coil breached the swells. Sunshine glanced off opalescent scales, casting a spray of blue and green light.

Buzz gasped. "What is it?"

"An overgrown sea slug," I drawled.

"A serpent?" Cairstine asked.

"Ol' Esmerelda. She lives in an underwater

cavern on Devil's Rock. I've never seen all of her at once, but she's at least three hundred feet from tip to tail." In a snap of suspicion, I wondered if Peter Pan was somehow behind the monster's attack.

"Whoa! That's enormous." Buzz fluttered his wings, lifting a few inches above his perch. "How long is *Revenge?*"

Cairstine clicked her teeth. "Half that."

"Oh." Buzz dropped to my wrist again.

In unison, the engineers asked, "What does she want with us?"

Cairstine added, "We don't have treasure in our holds."

"Good question, but I'm more concerned with stopping her. We have twenty-eight guns on board, but we might as well have none for all the good they'll do us against *that.*" I asked myself if I was paranoid for *wanting to* believe Pan was behind this. Everything wrong in life couldn't be blamed on the eternal boy...

Could it?

Ol' Esmerelda knocked again. The ship rocked and rolled, and we automatically adjusted our stances to compensate. The motion had become familiar. The conversation continued without interruption.

Buzz fluttered his wings. "Why are the guns useless?"

Wright beat me to the answer. "*Revenge* is blind and defenseless against attacks from below. The cannons can't be aimed into the water. So unless the serpent comes up against our sides, the artillery is ineffective."

"Hmm, not an effective design. We'll have to do something about that," Buzz mused, stroking his chin.

"Never mind that now. Focus on our immediate problem. Whatever is attacking us is beneath the ship. I need a solution, and I need it now," I said, but I doubt either of them heard me.

Wright bent to address the sprite. Her head blocked my view of him, so she appeared to be talking to my hook. "We need to find some means of delivering an explosive charge at depth."

Buzz's featherweight left my hook. He landed on Wright's shoulder, causing an unfamiliar feeling to stab me. It might've been jealousy, but that was impossible.

"The deeper the better," Buzz said. "Marine creatures have amazing hearing. They're susceptible to loud noises."

"A bomb with a long fuse might work, but we'll

need some way of keeping it dry." She tucked her face toward him, a habit I'd already acquired over the last couple hours.

"Carry on, then." I eased away, but I might as well have stomped for all the attention they paid me. Well, that'd gone better than expected. I wished the pair of them a prosperous and productive future together.

"Oh! Oh! Oh! I have an idea!" Buzz threw up his arms and his aura exploded into multi-colored sparkles.

"Tell me?" Wright rolled on the balls of her feet.

"Wine!" Buzz shouted. "We need a barrel of wine!"

In the clouds, a rooster crowed. "*Cock-a-doodle-doo!*"

CHAPTER 19

Doomed—Damning Decisions

Peter Pan swooped around the main mast and disappeared behind the sails, but his cocky cry resounded through the afternoon sky. "Cock-a-doodle-doo! Cock-a-doodle-doo! Cock-a-doodle-doo!"

"Argh." A growl rumbled from my throat. *That sound.* It grated on my nerves. I winced and ground my teeth. On reflex, I grabbed for the hilt of my cutlass. Steel hissed on leather, and the blade cleared the scabbard.

Buzz, still standing on Cairstine's shoulder, emitted a high-pitched squeak. His aura turned lime-green. "Jehoshaphat! It's Peter Pan! He's going to pluck my antenna and then my wings! I'm doomed. Dooooomed."

"Over my dead body. He'll have to come through me first." Wright drew her flintlock pistol and cocked the hammer.

Buzz hugged the curve of her neck. "My hero!"

Oh, what a pair. There was much I wanted to say, but sarcasm had to be denied for pragmatic reasons. "I'll deal with Pan. Wright, Buzz, return to your task."

Pan emerged from behind the mainsail and shot skyward. The higher he ascended, the smaller he appeared, until he receded to a bright green splotch. Sunlight glanced off the enchanted dagger he wielded. It was a tactic I recognized from previous encounters. When Peter reached the pinnacle, he would drop into a steep dive-attack.

Wright hesitated. "By task, you mean the sea serpent, Captain?"

"If you've any doubt, walk yourself off the plank." I kept my gaze pinned to Pan, craning my neck to follow him. The blinding sunlight forced me to squint and the position crimped my spine.

"Aye, aye, Captain." Wright hurried off, taking Buzz with her.

I settled into a fighting stance: weapons ready, legs braced, and knees bent. Tension thrummed through my frame. I kept my limbs limber, ready to pivot on my heel to meet his attack from any direction.

High above, Pan executed a swan dive, speeding so swiftly he appeared a green blur against the blue. I held my position for a critical second, assessing his trajectory. Peter flew arrow-true; I was the bullseye on the target.

Astonishment swelled through me. Temptation tugged. It flashed through my thoughts to stay put until the last possible moment and then step aside. Would he hit headfirst and knock himself senseless or punch a Pan-shaped hole in the planks? How many levels would he penetrate before he finally stopped? The matter was doomed to eternal speculation. I would never risk damaging my ship. Before the wonderance played out, I was already running.

Heart hammering against my chest, I sprinted toward the bow. The longboats and dinghy were stowed against the fo'c'sle bulwark. I drove with my knee, tucked my limbs, and hurtled onto the platform. Upon landing, my foot caught on something concealed beneath the tarp. I stumbled, struggling to recover my balance on the uneven surface.

In my peripheral vision, Pan streaked past off the port side, traveling parallel to my path. Playing cannonball with the main deck must not have appealed to him. It provided quite the impetus. Given the choice between a broken limb and Peter's dagger in my back, I preferred the former. To free my hand, I clenched my cutlass between my teeth. A headlong charge carried me into the next leap.

Not high enough this time. I smacked bodily against the bulwark. The collision knocked the wind from my lungs. My jaws clamped shut on the steel blade hard enough that my teeth ached.

My hand missed the balustrade, but my hook caught. I planted my boots, walked the wall, and hauled myself up and over. Before I cleared the railing, the hair on the back of my neck rose, and a thrill shot down my spine.

Gooseflesh rose on the back of my neck. *Danger!*

On pure instinct, I ducked and dropped. Before I hit the deck, Pan whooshed inches overhead. The point of his dagger sliced the air, and a blustery wind blasted across my back. The cutlass slipped from between my teeth. It clattered to the deck. Luckily, I didn't impale myself when I landed in a heap.

I crashed onto the fo'c'sle deck like a rogue wave, startling two members of my crew. The men shouted and fled. One jumped to the main deck, and the other dove head first through the open hatch.

Pan's reckless flight put him on a collision course with the foremast. I drew a sharp breath and hoped for a crash. At the last moment, he swerved sharply aside, but then flew straight into the ratlines and got entangled.

"Confound it!" Pan thrashed about within the net, struggling to free himself. Frantically, he sawed through hemp lines with his dagger. He was helpless. Trapped.

A perfect opportunity.

Where had that darned cutlass gone? I groped for the dropped weapon, and closed my hand on the blade. Sharp pain lanced my palm, but I barely noticed. The whole of my attention focused on my rival. I flipped the weapon around, secured a solid grip, and lunged straight for Pan.

He sliced the final rope and spilled from the net. My cutlass drove through the spot he'd been moments before. Missed again. A snarl churned in my chest.

Pan flopped on the deck, completely vulnerable.

I found myself caught in the gravity of irresistible

temptation. I could've run him through and finally ended our destructive rivalry. Denying myself that satisfaction was painful. It hurt, physically and spiritually, but I refrained, because Ol' Esmerelda was still a threat to *Revenge*.

I harbored no doubts that Pan had orchestrated the sea serpent's assault on my vessel. How he'd managed it remained in question. His murder, while satisfying, wouldn't necessarily guarantee the serpent would cease her attack. I couldn't kill him without unraveling the mystery, but that didn't mean I couldn't hurt him.

Pan started to rise.

"Oh no, you're not going anywhere." I drew back my boot and delivered a short, vicious kick to his side.

Peter groaned and bowled into the balustrade where he remained prostrate, clutching his ribs. Wheezing, he struggled to rise.

I planted my boot on his back and pushed him down. I needed those answers now, so I threw out a taunt. "That dive-bomb attack never works. Yet, you keep trying it."

"It's called 'death from above' and someday it'll be the end of you." He propped himself up on his elbows and glared, hatred in his gaze.

The feeling was mutual.

"Perhaps, but it seems more likely you'll brain yourself first." I could've explained to Peter why his "death from above" attack kept failing. Every time he attempted the maneuver, he ascended higher than the time before, which gave me more time to evade. Of course, I'm not stupid, so I kept my mouth shut.

An inconvenient jolt lifted the entire ship, throwing off my balance. Peter wormed out from beneath my foot. By the time I recovered my footing, he'd escaped. Pan somersaulted into flight and brought his enchanted knife into what he probably imagined to be a proper fencing position.

"On your guard, Hook!"

"*En garde.*" I assumed a ready stance with my cutlass raised, and our conflict resumed without a formal signal. Pan darted nearer and stabbed at my shoulder. I executed a smooth sidestep and countered.

Our blades clanged together.

The edges met and slid across one another with a hiss. When the weapons parted, I ducked beneath the dangling ratlines.

Peter pursued.

The fo'c'sle deck was a tight, cluttered space. We circled the mast, vying for the upper hand. Now,

Peter Pan and I shared an animosity well suited to embittered enemies. Our conflicts had certain unwritten, but mutually understood rules. In keeping with tradition, we sparred with words and weapons. For decades, we'd been evenly matched. I was taller and stronger, and despite his juvenile stature, Peter had faerie stamina and dexterity in excess. When combined with flight, he'd always managed to hold his own against me, and while it stung my pride to admit, he often bested me. Peter's recent growth spurt, however, had added a few inches to his height and bettered his reach. The difference threw off my rhythm, and he wasted no time in taking advantage of the vulnerability.

With a cry, he swung at my left side. I brought up my hook to parry, but miscalculated the angle. The dagger glanced off the vambrace that secured my hook. The stroke didn't damage the leather, but once it reached the top of the armor, the blade sank into my flesh and sliced a deep cut across the back of my forearm. Blood spurted from the wound, but my pride stung worse. I was angrier with myself than him over the lapse and I vowed it wouldn't happen again.

Peter claimed the victory. "First blood is mine and so shall be the victory!"

"Not so fast. I'm not dead yet." I set myself once more in the proper stance.

Peter thrust, I parried, and the fight resumed. He jeered. "You're still alive because I wish it. I could kill you now, Captain Hook. You are at my mercy."

"Ah, is that so?"

"It is, but I spared your life for the sake of Wendy." Peter tried to maneuver me into backing up into the open hatch. I wasn't falling for such trickery, especially not on my ship. This was *my* home turf. I had every plank committed to memory, right down to the knotholes.

"How thoughtful you are to consider the chit's feelings. Granted, we've only known one another a few hours, but I do believe Wendy has grown inordinately fond of me."

"Liar!" Peter's aura blazed, throwing a shower of fiery sparks. His face twisted into an ugly mask. He threw a wild thrust, leaving an opening in his guard.

The fervor of anger drove me into a powerful lunge. With an executioner's design, I heaved the cutlass at his throat. Peter sprang away in the nick of time. He caught hold of the mast with both hands and spun around it, kicked at me with both legs.

I spun and brought up my hook, intending to impale him. I reversed direction and brought up my hook a second time. Faerie intuition must've alerted Peter to the danger. He yelped and twisted, but not fast enough. The point sliced across his throat.

Pan dropped and squarely on the deck at my feet. Red oozed from the thin gash over his Adam's apple. Another inch and I'd have torn out his gullet. Peter swallowed convulsively. He looked about as astonished as I felt, but I doubt it was for the same reason. Surprise echoed through my mind, the same thought over and over. *Peter has an Adam's apple?* Boys grew them in puberty. It meant his physical age must've been at least eleven.

"Say, I do believe you're growing whiskers," I taunted, dueling with words as well as weapons. "At first I mistook that shadow on your upper lip for a spot of lint. But now I see it's definitely a mustache!"

Pan came at me in a frenzy, his silvery blade flashing. "Fibber! Wretch! Take that back!"

In the distance, activity caught my attention. I took the risk and stole a look over the top of Pan's head. The quarter deck was level with the fo'c'sle—a straight shot across the main deck. Wright and several members of the crew were in the middle of using the windlass to haul a dark oak cask out of the hold. Even at that distance, I recognized the vintage as elven wine, and worth a small fortune. *Dozens of barrels in the hold and they had to choose that specific one?* The thought of what they meant to do with it inspired genuine dread in my buccaneer's heart.

A wounded bellow rent my throat. "What in the blazes is going on?"

Ol' Esmerelda unleashed an unholy roar and dealt *Revenge* the most terrible blow yet. The serpent struck the midsection, a direct hit from below, and the entire ship bucked. I seized hold of the foremast to keep from falling.

Revenge groaned and quaked under the immense stress placed on her structure. From deep within the vessel came a series of sharp, successive *snaps*. Pressure built on my ribcage and I pressed my elbows to alleviate the crushing ache. I suffered right along with my beloved ship.

Peter gloated over my agony. "Your ship and the lives of everyone on board depend on me. I have a piece of Ol' Esmerelda's treasure hoard and she wants it back. She pursued me all the way from Devil's Rock. She'll sink your ship before she gives up."

I scoffed. "You expect me to believe she's making all this fuss over a bit of treasure? Your pockets are empty and so are your words."

"It's true!" Pan scowled fiercely. Predictably, the

insult got under his skin—he'd always hated being called a liar. He dug into his belt pouch. "The serpent wants *this!*"

Sunlight shone adoringly as it does on pure gold. The glow captured my attention. The sight of it sparked the ember of a memory of a tale I'd heard long ago, but there was no time for that now. At last, the cause of the wyrm's attack was revealed. Now I needed to remove the coin from his clutches and return it to Ol' Esmerelda. The urgency of acting before the serpent attacked again brought me to the edge of panic. It was impossible to think straight. *Revenge* had sustained internal damage. She couldn't survive another assault like the last.

"That's a Spanish doubloon. It's from the Otherworld," I said to buy myself time to think. I returned the cutlass to its sheath. "What would it be doing in the serpent's hoard?"

Perhaps sensing my intent, Peter increased the distance between us. He hovered over the middle of the main deck, well out of reach, and mockingly danced the coin across his knuckles. "I don't know, but there's a ton of 'em there. A Spanish king's ransom."

A Spanish king's ransom. Could the legend be

true? The possibility tantalized my imagination, but alas, there was no time for that now.

"Give it here," I demanded.

A slow, superior smile split his face. "I'll trade for it."

My gut clenched. I already knew the answer, but I asked anyway. "What do you want?"

"You know what I want. *Wendy*."

An impossible choice... My denial was automatic and adamant. "You can't have her."

"No? It's the girl or your ship, Hook. What's it going to be?"

At times, I suspected fate hated me. Wendy chose that exact moment to dash onto the main deck. In a flash of periwinkle, she scurried along the starboard railing, and not a single member of my preoccupied crew noticed her. Peter had his back to the stern and hadn't spotted the girl yet, either. Getting to Wendy first became an urgent priority, but the dilemma remained.

How was I to obtain that coin? I considered drawing a flintlock pistol and shooting Pan through the heart, but what if I missed or only wounded him? He might veer out over the ocean. The treasure could be lost to the depths...

Oh. Right. How stupid of me not to realize. To

return the doubloon, I'd have to toss it overboard anyway.

I grabbed for a pistol, drew and cocked it with the same action, and fired without aiming. Fire and smoke roared from the muzzle. The bullet struck Pan high on his right shoulder. He released a keening shriek and dropped straight to the deck. A surge of bloodthirsty satisfaction rushed through me.

Everyone who'd heard the shot turned to look. Wendy stumbled to a halt and covered her heart with her hand. She cried out, "Peter!"

Hurriedly, I freed a line and swung down to the main deck. The landing placed me between Pan and the girl. The second my boots struck the deck, I released the line and hit the ground running. My sense of priority was torn, but Wendy was right in front of me. She made for the obvious choice.

Mr. Brown flanked Wendy, trailing a couple paces behind her. I had no idea where he'd come from or how long he'd been there. Surprise broke my stride, and I slid to a stop a few feet from the two of them.

Wendy raised a cocked flintlock pistol. From its distinctive mother of pearl inlay and polished brass finish, I recognized it as Mr. Smee's stolen sidearm. She aimed the muzzle at my heart. "Halt right there,

Captain Hook! Get out of my way or I'll shoot you dead!"

"Your hands are shaking, girl. You don't have the mettle to pull the trigger." I stole an over-shoulder glance to where Pan rested in a heap of green on a pool of red. He twitched and groaned.

Still alive... darn.

"I'll do it. I will!" Wendy trembled like a newborn fawn.

"Miss Darling, please lower the weapon. You don't want to do this," Mr. Brown coached in a pleading voice. He edged nearer. His proximity raised gooseflesh on my nape. I disliked it immensely.

"Mr. Brown, back away. This is none of your concern." I waved him off, but the stubborn bard refused to obey. To present the greater threat, I strode toward Wendy. "Do you know what it means to live with blood on your hands—to become a murderer?"

"No, but you do," the girl said in a quavering voice.

"That's correct, I do, and believe me, it's not something you want." The distance closed to arm's length, so I reached for the pistol, intending to pluck it from her fingers.

"Stay away!" Wendy shrieked and flinched. She jerked her arms upward, aiming the muzzle at my face.

I slipped aside. What I failed to foresee, however, was Mr. Brown's burgeoning heroism. In a bid to save me, he threw himself in front of the gun. It all played out with surreal slowness, yet I found myself unable to act to stop it. A paralyzed witness, I watched in horror while the tragedy unfolded.

The pistol went off, and the shot struck Mr. Brown in the chest. Red splashed across his white tunic. He staggered, clutching his wound, and toppled. Wendy shrieked and cast away the smoking gun, but too damn late for it to do anyone a lick of good.

"Wendy, run! Come here quick!" Pan shouted from behind me.

"Peter!" Wendy raised her chin. Hope lit her sweet face. *Foolish girl.* She gathered herself and bolted toward Pan. If she were smart, she'd have fled from him.

Wrath ruled me, an all-consuming flame that consumed me from within. I lashed out, caught hold of Wendy's arm, and wrenched her off her feet. She cried out, but I was uncaring of her pain. I only had concern for my own terrible grief and anger.

Grasping the girl, I swung around. Peter hovered five feet off the deck in spite of his injury. He had his fist clenched shut, which meant he still had the coin... or was pretending. My instincts said he did. I settled my hook against Wendy's tender throat and snarled, "Give me the coin or I'll end her."

Peter's jaw dropped, but then his gaze sparked. He held up the doubloon. "Even trade, the girl for the coin?"

"Even trade. No tricks. Your word of honor."

"No trickery. You have my word on it." Pan raised his hand in pledge.

"On my honor, I swear to exchange the girl for the coin," I freely spoke the words that would damn me forever—and I cared not, because Mr. Brown's blood stained the deck of my ship. Concern for Wendy's welfare no longer troubled me. I cared only for my ship and my crew.

The girl must go, or I'd kill her myself. She must go or I'd break my promise to Buzz and desecrate everything I'd fought for my entire life.

Pan tossed the coin. "Catch."

I snatched it from the air and shoved Wendy so she stumbled toward him. Low and vicious, I hissed, "You deserve what's coming to you, girl."

Wendy gasped and recoiled. Through the haze

of hatred, I couldn't see her face. Later, when I recreated the moment in my imagination, however, the girl gaped at me in pure horror.

Pan seized Wendy's hand and fled with his prize. I turned my back and didn't watch them leave. I rushed to Mr. Brown and sank to my knees. His blood soaked the fabric of my trousers. I gripped his shoulder, turned him over, and gathered him into my embrace.

Mr. Brown gasped for breath with red spittle bubbling on his lips. His gaze locked on my face and he wheezed my name, "Captain Hook..."

My throat ached, and tightness constricted my chest. My eyes bled. Moisture trickled down my cheeks and I wondered when it had started raining. "Why did you do this damnable stupid thing, Virgil?"

"You were kind to me." Virgil raised trembling hands and I caught them between my own. He resisted my efforts to still his shaking. When I glanced down, I saw he was trying to remove his ruby ring.

"What are you doing, old man?"

"Captain Hook, I want you to have this." He finally managed to slip the ring off and made a clumsy effort to place it on my middle finger. I assisted him, even though my first instinct was to object.

I didn't deserve it.

Virgil wheezed. "It fits."

"Thank you," I whispered, blinded by tears.

"Thank you, Jayden." Virgil smiled and breathed his last.

On the main deck, a beast roared in the throes of torment. The sound chilled my soul. I pitied that monstrous fiend, and I vowed to put it out of its misery.

Virgil became music when he died. His fingers transformed into the strokes of a five-line staff, which flowed as twin ribbons into the air. The change claimed his arms next and his pure spirit painted the notes on the scrolling staves. The most beautiful music I'd heard in my entire life filled the heavens—a celestial orchestra. His body lost substance. I hugged him tighter, trying to keep him with me, but eventually emptiness filled my arms.

Mr. Brown has haunted me ever since. His passing is my greatest regret.

Pride and Piracy

A deafening explosion rousted me from my grief-stricken torpor. It emanated from off the starboard side. A shower of seawater rained onto the deck seconds later, drenching me to the skin. I heaved to my feet and strode to where Wright and a crowd of crewmembers gathered against the railing.

They parted before me, clearing a path to the balustrade. Only Wright, with Buzz perched on her shoulder, held her ground. I settled fist and hook on the taffrail and gazed into the sea.

Ol' Esmerelda's limp, serpentine form floated in

the water. Only three coiled sections of the immense sea serpent thrust above the surface. Aqua scales glittered with opalescent beauty. I had no idea how my engineers had managed it, but they'd saved the ship. I was amazed, thankful, and proud.

"Is it dead or stunned?" I asked in a croak.

Buzz's wings hummed, and he skipped to my shoulder. "Your guess is as good as mine, but I suggest we get the fig roll out of here before it wakes up."

"An excellent suggestion. Make it so."

No one moved.

I filled my lungs and roared, "I gave an order! To your posts or I'll send you to the sharks!"

They scattered and scurried away. Weak-kneed, I clung to the railing for support. Buzz stayed with me. He hugged my neck, explaining the intricacies of constructing the "depth charge" that'd saved the ship. Best of all, he said *nothing* about Wendy—no condemnation or accusation. When I vomited over the side, he held my hair aside. To him, I was eternally grateful.

Eventually, Ol' Esmerelda sank below the waves.

Time passed, and my stomach calmed. *Revenge* turned into the blustery headwind we'd fought for so long and so hard to reach this cursed place. Formerly the enemy, now our ally, the easterly breeze filled our sails.

We traveled less than a quarter mile before the call came from the crow's nest. "There's a ship off our aft!"

I strode to the ship's rear and ascended through the sterncastle to where a bruised and battered Mr. Smee met me on the poop deck. I aimed my spyglass at the horizon.

The graceful profile of a schooner skipped across the breakers at what must've been a staggering eighteen knots. It was, unmistakably, *Ariel.* The warmth of relief melted some of the ice that encased my heart. Then delight bubbled through me because Starkey was alive.

Ariel maintained her northern bearing, moving away from us. Mr. Smee sputtered in his outrage, "Starkey has stolen the schooner!"

"Well," I said dryly. "I never saw *that* coming."

"Shall we pursue?" Smee asked.

I scoffed. "Don't be absurd, Mr. Smee. We have not a chance of catching her. That ship is a clipper. See how she uses her sails."

"This is mutiny, Captain."

A scowl contorted my countenance. "Use the precise and correct terminology, Mr. Smee. That ship has never been under my command. Obviously, this is an act of piracy committed by pirates under the command of a pirate captain."

I was damn proud of Starkey.

Smee frowned and worked his mouth. Clearly, he didn't comprehend the distinction. It didn't matter, because *I* understood. The bo'sun stroked his chin. "We're not to pursue?"

"Set our course for Rackham's Cay, Mr. Smee. We'll put in for repairs there." Eventually, I'd catch up with Starkey, but not today or tomorrow. I wished him well and smooth sailing, and hoped he enjoyed his joy ride to the fullest. In the meanwhile, more urgent matters demanded my immediate attention.

"Advise our engineers to ready the bilge pumps. We're taking on water."

Mr. Smee scowled, obviously wondering how and what I thought I knew. The bo'sun shared not even the slightest thread of rapport with *Revenge.* Thankfully, he didn't argue, only saluted, and passed the orders along.

"Aye, aye." Smee descended to the helm.

We'd be lucky to put into port before we sank.

I held a long vigil for Mr. Brown on the deck, and mourned the music yet unperformed. The sun set. Eventually, the fact that I still clutched that pilfered doubloon impinged on my awareness. I held it up for inspection. A red-brown crust coated the coin.

Blood money now.

Cursed gold bought more trouble than it was worth, so I cast that doubloon into the sea. If I never laid eyes on it again, it'd be too soon.

The End.

ABOUT THE AUTHOR

Melissa Snark is a fantasy and romance author. She lives in Anacortes, Washington with her husband, three children and a glaring of cats.

Join Melissa Snark's newsletter to be notified of new releases.

For more information...
www.melissasnark.com
melissasnark@melissasnark.com

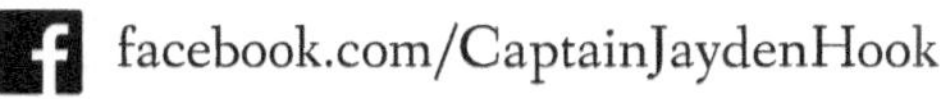 facebook.com/CaptainJaydenHook

Captain Hook & the Pirates of Neverland

Hook: Dead to Rights (Book #1)

Hook: Dead Wrong (Book #2)

Hook: Death Wish (Book #3)

Loki's Wolves Universe

Ragnarök: Doom of the Gods Series

Valkyrie's Vengeance (Book #1)

Hunger Moon (Book #2)

Battle Cry (Book #3)

Wolf's Cross (Book #4)

Hunter's Mark (Book #5/Prequel)

Sassafras Shifters

A Cat's Tale (Book #1)

Out Foxed (Book #2)

A Very Foxy Christmas (short story) in Christmas Kisses anthology

That Old Black Magic Universe

Heart's Desired Mate Series

Love is the Law

A Novel of the Fallen Angels

Prophecy

Aries Cursed series

(A Zodiac Shifters Book)

Ram Rugged by Melissa Thomas

The Bonded (short story) in Crimson Kisses anthology

How to Tame Your Dragon Mate series

(A Zodiac Shifters Book)

Bewitched Dragon Mates by Melissa Thomas